Angel's Devil

Dragging Angelique, the mastiff changed directions to lunge after another bird. Angel spun around and slammed hard into someone. Startled, she tried to push away, but Brutus bounded behind them, tangling them in his leash and effectively binding them together.

Angelique shut her eyes. "I'm so sorry," she mumbled into a broad chest.

"In some African tribes, this would make us married," a dry male voice returned.

Angel looked up. A tall, lean man with windswept black hair looked down at her with amused emerald eyes. "In others, it would mean we're being prepared for supper," she returned, suddenly less upset than she had been a moment before.

Her fellow captive grinned. "So is it matrimony, or shall I attempt to untangle us?"

Angel's Devil

SUZANNE ENOCH

AVON BOOKS  NEW YORK

ANGEL'S DEVIL is an original publication of Avon Books. This work has never before appeared in book form. This work is a novel. Any similarity to actual persons or events is purely coincidental.

AVON BOOKS
A division of
The Hearst Corporation
1350 Avenue of the Americas
New York, New York 10019

Copyright © 1995 by Suzanne Enoch
Published by arrangement with the author
Library of Congress Catalog Card Number: 95-94310
ISBN: 0-380-78023-2

First Avon Books Printing: November 1995

AVON TRADEMARK REG. U.S. PAT. OFF. AND IN OTHER COUNTRIES, MARCA REGISTRADA, HECHO EN U.S.A.

Printed in the U.S.A.

RA   10   9   8   7   6   5   4   3   2   1

For my parents, Joan and Lee,
who have always encouraged me
to use my imagination in all things

And for my Aunt Vivian,
who dreamed about this the night before it happened

1

"**P**apa, I don't remember that we had this much luggage in Calais."

Angelique Graham frowned as yet another dock worker appeared, a stack of hat boxes in his arms. With France still torn and wounded by the ambitions of Bonaparte, going shopping in Paris had seemed rather frivolous to her, but her mother and Lady Penston had made the most of the opportunity. And as the women had now strolled up to the shops at the head of the Dover pier while they waited for the coaches to be loaded, undoubtedly they were intent on making still more purchases.

Thomas Graham, the Earl of Niston, chuckled at her. "I do hope two coaches are enough for us and your mother's things."

Angel smiled. "I know. If we'd stayed any longer we'd need an entire caravan."

Her father guided her a few steps away from Lord Penston, who was busily directing the loading of their respective coaches. "Your mother's already talking about making another trip before your wedding," he said in a low voice. "I believe she has her heart set on you walking down the aisle in a French gown."

Angelique sighed. "If you would let me marry Simon right away, she could have found one this trip."

1

Niston glanced over at the baron. "Angel, we explained that already. A year is hardly an unusual period of time to wait between an engagement and a wedding."

"But Simon and I want to be married now," she protested. "You know that."

Niston put a hand on her shoulder. "And you know that nine months isn't that long."

"But you won't even let us announce it!"

"We want you to be certain of your decision before we make a public declaration," he said soothingly.

"You mean you don't think I'll go through with it, and you don't want to be embarrassed when I change my mind," she countered.

He frowned, obviously running out of patience. "We think no such—"

"Well, I won't change my mind," Angelique stated. "Simon and I are in love."

"Thomas," Lord Penston interrupted, "is that yours, or Nora's?" He pointed at one of the packages.

"Yours. I think." Her father stepped over to examine it.

The baron nodded, summoning another dock worker. "I say, boy, that package goes in the other carriage. No, that box, the one over there, by the wheel."

At the sound of dogs barking Angelique turned in the direction of the water, where several ships were being loaded for the return to Calais. Two kennelmen guided a pack of hounds up one of the ramps. A third man stood at the foot of the gangplank, wrestling with another half dozen dogs. One of them, a brown mastiff bigger and bulkier than the lively hounds, was obviously reluctant to board the ship. The handler hit the animal across the back with a knobbed wooden staff, and the dog yelped.

Scowling furiously, Angelique hiked up her skirts and dashed past a cart stacked with squawking chickens, and stalked up to the kennelman. "Stop that at once!" she commanded.

He straightened to give her a surly look. "What's that?"

"Stop striking that animal! Can't you see it's merely frightened?"

The man gave the dog's leash a hard yank, and the animal let out a howl. "The mutt's a watchdog, miss. It ain't supposed to be frightened."

"Fenley!" A well-dressed man leaned over the railing above them. "What's the delay? Get those dogs on board immediately!"

"Aye, milord," Fenley returned. "It's only this blasted brute keeping us." He glowered and raised the stick again.

Incensed, Angel swung her reticule at him. The bag, containing several metal-cast soldiers for her brother, struck him hard in the arm.

"Why, you—!" Fenley protested, raising one hand to ward her off.

"You are not to hit that dog!" Angel snapped.

The mastiff looked up at her and gave one pitiful wag of its drooping tail.

"Is something amiss, my lady?" the man called down.

"Yes! This man insists on beating this poor creature simply because it's afraid."

The man stroked his moustache. "You must understand, my lady, we sail with the tide."

"That is no excuse for brutality," she returned.

A group of soldiers behind her was exchanging coins, and the nearest dockworkers had set down their loads to watch the amusement.

"You are correct. My apologies." The man looked at his kennelman. "Fenley, give her the leash. My lady, thank you for your concern. I am certain Brutus will be more content in your care than in mine." He doffed his hat. "Good day."

Angelique watched, somewhat stunned, as Fenley untangled the mastiff's leash and handed it over to her. "Glad to be rid of ye, ye stupid mutt," he snarled. The animal growled at him.

The other dogs bounded up the ramp and into the ship. Angelique looked down at her new charge. "Oh, my," she muttered. Brutus wagged his tail at her.

The soldiers laughed and more coins were exchanged, though she couldn't imagine what they might be wagering on this time. With a grimace, she wrapped the leash around her wrist and tugged. Mama and Papa weren't going to like this. Her brother and sister had been wanting a dog, though, and they would simply have to understand. Brutus fell in beside her, and they headed back toward the carriages.

Halfway there the mastiff spotted the crates of chickens. With a thunderous bark he was off, dragging Angelique behind him. It was all she could do to stay on her feet. "Brutus, stop!" The dog bounded atop the nearest crate, smashing it open. A dozen chickens exploded out onto the pier, Brutus after every one of them. "Brutus, no!" she yelled.

The mastiff changed directions to lunge after another bird. Angel spun around, and slammed hard into someone. Startled, she tried to push away, but Brutus bounded behind them, tangling them in his leash and effectively binding them together. Angelique shut her eyes for a moment.

"I'm so sorry," she mumbled into a broad chest. Her mother was going to be furious.

"In some African tribes, this would make us married," a dry male voice returned.

Angel looked up. His arms reflexively gripping her waist, a tall, lean man with windswept black hair looked down at her with amused emerald eyes. "In others, it would mean we're being prepared for supper," she returned, abruptly less upset than she had been a moment earlier.

The man grinned. "Your dog seems quite determined."

"He's just barely my dog," Angel admitted, tugging at the leash in a vain effort to rein in the barking mastiff.

"I saw," her fellow captive returned. "So is it matrimony, or shall I attempt to untangle us?"

Angel grinned back at him, relieved that he wasn't angry. "Untangling for the moment, I think. We can discuss the rest once we've been introduced."

Green eyes dancing, her rescuer freed the leash from her wrist and then hauled on the braided leather. With a surprised woof Brutus sat back on his haunches, and taking Angel through two quick turns elegant enough to be worthy of Almack's assembly, the stranger had them free. He scratched Brutus's head when the canine stood and wagged its tail at him. "I knew there was a reason I should sail back to England today. James Faring, at your service."

"Thank you for your assistance, Mr. Faring," Angel replied, smoothing her rumpled blue muslin skirt. From his dress and manner of speech her rescuer was obviously a member of the upper classes, but she was positive he hadn't attended any of the Season's events. She would certainly remember having met James Faring.

"My pleasure," he replied, inclining his head. "After your brave rescue of . . ." He gestured at the mastiff.

"Brutus," she supplied, grinning.

"Of Brutus," he repeated, "it seemed the least I could do to perform my own." He grinned ruefully. "Though I was a bit tardy, I'm afraid."

"No one was killed, or eaten, so I believe you were in time."

He laughed. "If I may ask, what is a young lady of quality doing alone in Dover?"

"I'm not alone," Angel corrected, guiltily glancing about for her father.

"Not any longer." He grinned at her again. "After all, we are practically engaged, are we not?"

"And after such a short courtship," she returned smoothly.

"But a very entertaining one."

Entertaining or not, if one of the patronesses of Almack's had viewed any of this incident she would be banned from the Assembly for life. And aside from that, she remembered belatedly, a lady, and especially an engaged one, did not converse with strange men. "Excuse me. I must be going."

She reached for Brutus's leash, but Mr. Faring shook his head. "Please, allow me to complete my rather pitiful rescue attempt," he requested, and motioned her to lead the way.

"Are you certain?" Angel queried, relieved that she

wouldn't have to haul the mastiff across the remainder of the pier.

"It is my infinite pleasure." He fell into step with her, Brutus beside him.

He was limping. "Did I—we—do that?" she queried, dismayed.

James Faring grimaced. "No. That is from a different rescue entirely."

"You often come to the aid of dazed and overwhelmed women, then?" she returned lightly.

"Only ones as thoroughly charming as you. You are an angel."

Angel chuckled. "And how did you know that, Mr. Faring?" she queried, raising an eyebrow.

Mr. Faring looked nonplussed, but before he could respond, Lord Penston and her father arrived.

"James Faring," the baron cried, extending his hand. "Jamie, it's good to see you. They placed bets at White's on the time and place of your demise, you know."

James Faring returned the handshake, but this time his smile didn't quite reach his eyes. "Old Bonie had a go at me, that's for certain," he replied. "It'll be good to get home." He glanced over at the line of carriages waiting for passengers at the edge of the teeming pier. "My transportation, however, doesn't appear to have arrived." He grimaced. "Looks as though I'll be hiring a hack."

So he had fought under Wellington. The bulk of the army had returned to England more than a month ago, though, and she couldn't imagine what he had been doing still in France. He wasn't in uniform, but wore a well-cut gray jacket and breeches and a pair of excellent quality Hessian boots, a large paw print currently marring the perfect polish of one of them.

Angel glanced up in the direction of the shops as her mother and the baroness emerged from a doorway and started toward them. She looked down at the happily panting Brutus. Whatever excuse she gave, her mother would still be appalled at her new acquisition and at her subsequent behavior, and no doubt she would hear about her irresponsibility and impulsiveness all the way back to London.

"You must ride with us," she offered brightly, avoiding her father's startled look. Having a guest in the coach would do wonders in keeping her mother's tirade to a minimum.

"That's right," the baron seconded helpfully. "Thomas has a good team. Better than a bloody hired hack." The stout man glanced over at Angel's father. "Damn me and my manners. Just so surprised to see you alive, lad. This is Thomas Graham, the Earl of Niston, and his daughter, Angelique. Thomas, Jamie Faring, the Marquis of—"

"James," James Faring, the Marquis of Something, interrupted. He shook her father's hand. "And we've met, I believe?"

"Several years ago, yes," Angel's father intoned. "Never had a chance to convey my condolences about your father. He was a good man."

The marquis nodded. "Yes, he was. Thank you."

Niston glanced over at his daughter. "Saw what happened. Thank you for assisting my Angel." Despite his words he didn't look pleased, and Angel wondered whether it was Brutus or her invitation that had put him out of sorts.

"My pleasure." The amused smile returned to James Faring's lips, and to his eyes. "So you are indeed an Angel."

Her mother and Lady Penston had reached them, yet another stack of packages in tow. Her mother's look of trepidation at their new acquaintance was even more pronounced than her father's had been, and Angel wondered for a moment if the marquis would get her in more trouble than the dog was likely to.

The marquis nodded to the women and stepped closer to Angel. "If you'll excuse me," he said, apparently sensing that his welcome was less than assured, "I'd best be on my way." He offered the end of the leash to her, his eyes catching hers as their fingers brushed.

Angel's father cleared his throat. "My daughter is correct. You would be welcome to accompany us," he offered. "As Penston said, while my horseflesh might not measure up to your standards, my coach is considerably more well-sprung than a hack.''

"Your team is splendid," Angel cut in indignantly. She had helped pick them out, after all.

Her father smiled. "But we are speaking to a man who owns one of the finest stables in England." He motioned at the marquis. "My lord?"

"I, ah . . ." James glanced over at Angelique and gave a slight smile. "I would be grateful." He gestured behind him. "Just let me get my bag."

"I'm surprised he's even standing," the baron muttered as the marquis limped back toward the end of the pier.

"Why do you say that?" Angel asked.

"His position was overrun at Waterloo," Penston answered, "and he was mad enough to stand his ground. First rumor was that he was dead, second was that he'd live, but he'd lost an arm and a leg. Devil's own luck, that one."

The baron and baroness headed for their carriage, while her father filled in her mother about Angel's rescue of Brutus and helped them both into their own coach. Without coaxing, Brutus jumped in and lay at her feet. Camellia, Lady Niston, glared at the animal; then, obviously feeling there was something more pressing that needed her attention, turned on her husband. "Thomas, I can't believe you offered that man a ride to London in our carriage," she snapped.

Niston leaned up into the coach. "He saved Angel from being dragged all over Dover, Cammy."

That sent Camellia's gaze in her daughter's direction. "That's right, young lady. I don't know why we bothered to hire that endless string of governesses for you when you can't seem to remember for longer than two minutes how to behave like a lady. I shudder to think how Simon Talbott would react to seeing you like this. Now perhaps you understand why we insisted you wait a year before your wedding, and why we've refrained from announcing the engagement. This outrageous behavior must stop. And that . . . dog must go."

That hardly seemed fair, and there had only been seven or

eight stuffy governesses, not an endless string, as her mother so frequently exaggerated. "Simon wouldn't mind. And Brutus—"

"A lady does not shout, nor does she fling her reticule, or her skirts, about for the world to view," her mother cut in.

"What was I supposed to do, then?" Angel protested.

Lady Niston glared at her daughter. "Nothing."

"Nothing?" Angelique repeated incredulously. "That deuced—"

"Angel!" her mother admonished.

"That awful man," she amended unwillingly, "was hitting Brutus."

"That is beside the point," her mother returned, ignoring Angel's exasperated expression. "When a lady is given a choice between being involved in a scandal and doing nothing, she does nothing."

"I did *not* cause a scandal," Angel retorted. "I saved a poor, frightened dog."

"And conversed with a man to whom you had not been introduced. You might have been ruined."

Angel rolled her eyes. "The marquis thought I was right in acting, so there's no harm done."

Her mother scoffed. "Oh, yes there is. You've put yourself in debt to a gentleman of extreme ill repute."

"But who is he?" Angel entreated.

"The Marquis of Abbonley."

Angel blanched. With that lean build and those fascinating emerald eyes, James Faring had looked like a hero out of some romantic fable. She'd had no idea who he truly was. No wonder her parents were so dismayed. "The Devil?" she whispered.

"Exactly so," her father answered, frowning. "The Devil himself."

"But he's . . ." Angel trailed off, realizing that her life had just become a great deal more complicated. "He's Simon's cousin."

2

The Earl of Niston had told the truth. His coach was considerably more well-sprung than a damned hired hack. If not for the Graham parents' stiff-backed disapproval and his still-aching wounds, James decided that he might have enjoyed his return to London. As it was, though, he was relieved that Brutus was along to accept a portion of the poorly disguised hostility.

The wisest decision would undoubtedly have been to stay in Dover for another few days. His welcome in London had never been the most certain of things, anyway, though in the past he hadn't much cared. But it was time to reform, to see if he could finally become respectable. He'd been away for over a year this time, and after what Wellington and Napoleon had put him through, the *ton*'s token demon was ready to settle down.

He glanced speculatively over at Angel. The simplest and most obvious way to demonstrate that he had mended his ways would be to find a wife. And to be perfectly honest, Angelique Graham seemed more lively, and certainly more interesting, than the docile and demure female he had envisioned for himself. She was a beauty, with her copper hair and impossibly long-lashed bright hazel eyes, and he had been quite unable to resist rushing to her rescue.

10

The Earl of Niston cleared his throat. "How'd you come to return to England today?" he queried.

"Doctor only let me out of bed a week ago," James returned. He shrugged, the motion pulling at the tender scar on his left shoulder. "Today was the first day I thought I could make it."

That seemed to signal Lady Niston to begin what his grandmother had deemed goose-down prattle, feathery-light and meaningless conversation that required no response and that seemed to drift out of thought as soon as the words were spoken. Camellia Graham was an *artiste*. The younger Graham female twiddled her fingers, gazed out the small window, and looked over at him several times, obviously as bored as he. Finally, she became engrossed in stitching some sort of design onto a handkerchief, no small feat in the lurching coach. The tip of her tongue protruded from one side of her lips in concentration.

"What are you making, Lady Angelique?" he ventured when the mother had to pause to take a breath.

She looked up at him. "Roses," she answered, leaning forward to show him and giving him what would have been a superb view of her bosom if he had been feeling so inclined as to look.

"Very nice," he muttered, glancing at her mother.

"You didn't even look," Angelique protested, sitting back again.

"I did."

"You didn't." She examined her handiwork again. "They are a bit crooked, I'm afraid."

"Angelique," Lady Graham rebuked.

James stifled a smile. "They're lovely." The coach rocked through yet another rut, and he hissed. The dog looked up at him and wagged its tail.

"Do you wish to stop for a bit?" the countess asked.

He shook his head tightly, concentrating on taking deep breaths. "I'm fine."

"Don't be a nodcock," Angel snapped, her voice and expression concerned. "You look horrid."

"Well, thank you very much," he retorted. No one had ever dared call him a nodcock before, and he wasn't certain he liked it.

"Angel!" her mother admonished again.

"I'm trying to be nice," she protested.

Thus far her attempts at propriety hadn't seemed to be going very well. They had something in common, then. "Be nice to someone else," he suggested tightly.

The earl cleared his throat. "Excuse me, Abbonley, but I hardly think it's appropriate for you to speak to my daughter in that manner."

James looked sideways at him.

"You know," the countess began before he had decided how diplomatically to word his reply, "that reminds me of a particularly amusing *on dit* I heard several weeks ago about the Duke of Kent."

"Oh, really?" James responded, forcing his lips into what he hoped would pass for a smile.

"Yes. It seemed he . . ."

James lost track of what the countess was saying as he glanced over at Angelique. She crossed her eyes at him, and he coughed to cover his surprised and amused chuckle.

After another agonizing two hours of rutted roads and excruciating conversation, the coach rolled to a halt in front of Faring House. When James stepped to the ground, his bad leg, stiff from the long sit, gave way, and he had to hang onto the door handle to keep from falling. Brutus stood, apparently ready to follow him, but the girl hauled on the leash and the dog sat again.

"A pleasure, Lady Angelique," James murmured, looking up at her. "Perhaps we shall meet again."

She returned his smile. "I'm certain we shall, my lord."

"Thank you, Niston, my lady," he nodded.

"Very good," the earl muttered, and in a moment the coach rumbled out of the drive. James sighed. With the exception of Miss Graham, and Brutus, that had been agonizing. Hopefully the remainder of proper London society would be less trying.

"My God," came a voice from the townhouse doorway, and he looked up to see his cousin coming toward him at a run. "Jamie!"

"Simon," the marquis replied, grinning, and found himself pulled into a careful embrace. "I won't break," he growled.

With a chuckle Simon tightened his grip and thumped him on the back. "You look half dead," his cousin commented. "By God, I'm pleased to see you."

"Steady, Simon. I'm not exactly in sterling condition, either."

"Why didn't you write that you were returning?" his cousin complained, releasing him. "We were worried about you, you know. Those damn rumors from Belgium, and the—"

"I did write. And believe me, I've heard all about the wagering and the pish-posh about the Devil's due. It's good to see you again." He gripped his cousin's shoulder.

"Who was it that brought you back?" Simon asked. "I owe them a debt."

James grinned. "An angel rescued me and flew me home."

Simon grimaced. "We'd best get you inside. I believe you're delirious."

The marquis chuckled. "It was the Earl of Niston and his family."

"Niston?" Simon started, then gave a grin of his own. "Oh, *that* Angel. I'm glad you've met her. Isn't she wonderful?"

"Yes, she is. In fact—" James stopped, frowning and abruptly suspicious. "You're hardly the type to send innocents in my direction. Why are you glad I've met her," he queried, "and why is it I have the feeling I'm missing something here?"

His cousin looked at him for a moment. "They didn't say anything, did they?" he sighed. "I'm glad you've met her because, come next April, I'll be married to her."

James let go of his cousin's shoulder and straightened,

despite the wave of dizziness that ran through him. "Married?" he echoed, raising an eyebrow and carefully suppressing his abrupt disappointment. "You?"

"I'm not the one who's sworn off marriage," Simon pointed out. "That was you. And we'll discuss it later." His cousin grabbed James as his knees gave way. "You sapskull," Simon growled, as he motioned the butler to come out from the doorway. "You must have been rowing with one oar to try to get back here now. You could have waited a few more weeks, for Lucifer's sake."

"I've been away long enough." With that the last of his strength gave out. As he sagged into Simon's grip, his cousin began yelling for the servants to come help because the marquis was finally home.

"Just like you to sleep through a family reunion, Jamie."

His eyes snapped open. Elizabeth, the Dowager Viscountess Wansglen, sat by the bed, a cup of tea in her hand and a book on the table beside her. "Grandmama," he smiled, delighted, but when he tried to sit up she motioned him back with a quick wave that nearly sent the tea cascading over the bed sheets.

"Oh, bother," she muttered, and set the cup down. "You've turned me into a bundle of nerves, child."

Grandmama Elizabeth was the only person who to his knowledge still referred to him as a child. "That wasn't my intention," he responded.

"Then what was your intention, coming home without letting anyone know? You might have written a letter. Instead we get your trunks, your valet, and a note saying, 'I'll be home when I can.' Simon said you were half dead when you arrived. You know better than to be so foolish."

James grinned. "Still haven't given up railing at me, have you? And I did write. Blame the London Mail, not me."

Unexpectedly, the dowager viscountess leaned forward and kissed him on the cheek. "I missed you horribly, Jamie. Simon always listens to me when I scold him."

He laughed. "When have you ever scolded Simon?"

Elizabeth Talbott smiled. "You were both wicked boys. Simon grew out of it."

James's smile faded. It was true he had grown up wild after the death of his mother, just before his sixth birthday. He had driven governesses to distraction and to positions elsewhere on a regular basis, and later only just escaped being sent down from Cambridge when he and Viscount Luester decided a brawl was the best way to decide the question of which of them owned a certain lady's heart. The answer to that question, though, wasn't ultimately decided until a year later with a duel in a damp, fog-shrouded meadow. A duel that had given him the nickname of Devil.

He glanced away. "Simon told me he's engaged."

She nodded. "Yes, to Angelique Graham. She's a lovely sprite, and Simon's convinced she's a gift from heaven. Her daft parents, though, want to keep the whole thing a secret."

"What in the world for?"

"Oh, you'll have to ask Simon," she grumbled. "They don't think she's settled enough for him, or some rot." Her expression changed slightly. "But then you've met her, haven't you?"

"Yes, I have." He frowned as she eyed him over the rim of her cup. "What's that look for?"

"Nothing."

"Oh," he retorted. "I see. I set eyes on Simon's betrothed, and you think I'll attempt something scandalous."

"No, I don't. I was just wondering . . . if you'd changed your mind about marrying."

"I've been asking myself the same question, actually," he admitted after a moment. "It does rather seem to be past time for it."

His grandmother practically glowed. "Oh, Jamie, that's wonderful. And you said you'd sworn off the institution. Who is sh—"

"So," he interrupted, "as I've been gone for over a year and don't know who's available, I would appreciate if you'd put together a list of eligible females. I would prefer someone quiet, with a respectable background. I don't really care about age, or looks, but I would prefer if she wasn't completely dim and didn't squint.''

Grandmama Elizabeth sat back slowly. ''Are you looking for a bride, or a horse?'' she queried after a moment.

James snorted and struggled upright. ''You're the one who keeps nagging at me to find a wife, settle down, have children, and stop behaving like the Devil himself.''

''But . . . don't you wish to find someone you care for? You're going about it as if it's a business proposition.''

''Isn't it? You know damned well that the number of marriages made out of social or monetary necessity far outnumber the supposed love matches,'' he returned cynically.

Elizabeth stood, picking up her book and her tea. ''I am not going to assist you in this, James. You are one of the few people in the enviable position of being able to marry for love. I'll not be a party to your wasting that.''

''I'd be wasting my time if I waited for such nonsense.''

She turned around. ''You are wrong, James. You're only saying that because of Desiree. It's been—''

''Don't mention that . . . woman's name in my presence,'' he snapped.

''I only hope you realize what a mistake you're making before it's too late for you and whatever unfortunate girl you select.''

''Well, we'll see, won't we?'' he returned, sitting back again and annoyed that the one female who came to mind apparently wasn't available.

''Yes, I imagine we will,'' his grandmother replied as she left the room.

''Brutus,'' Angel complained as the dog pulled her across the edge of Hyde Park, ''if you can't mind me, Mama and Papa will never let you stay.''

Whether he understood or not, Brutus left off sniffing a promising clump of shrubs and returned to her side. Angel's maid, Tess, gave a relieved sigh. ''I still think we should have brought one of the grooms, my lady,'' she commented.

"If that dog takes it into his head to make off with you, I'll never be able to catch up."

Angel nodded, agreeing. "I know, but he doesn't seem to like men holding his leash. I think it's because that awful man, Fenley, was so mean to him." She tugged on the line, and Brutus turned to follow them as they toured the edge of the Ladies' Mile, hopefully far enough from the track that the mastiff wouldn't be tempted to chase any of the horses cantering there.

"I wish you'd warned me about the danger of reining him in before I attempted such a perilous feat myself," a voice came from behind her, and she turned around.

"My lord," she said with a surprised smile, as James Faring approached across the grass. He was on foot, as she was, a gold-tipped cane in one hand.

Brutus gave a woof and bounded toward the marquis. Tail wagging furiously, the dog jerked Angelique helplessly forward. "Oh, not again," she muttered, hauling with all her might on the leash. Despite her best efforts they careened full speed toward Abbonley.

"No, Brutus," the marquis stated firmly as the dog reached him. Immediately Brutus collapsed at Lord Abbonley's feet. James leaned over and scratched him behind the ears.

"Thank goodness," Angelique sighed, grinning at the marquis. "Apparently you are considered part of the rescue party, and are acceptable to him."

"Thank goodness, indeed," he muttered, straightening. Eyes twinkling, he reached out to take her free hand and bring it to his lips.

The marquis still looked pale and tired, but then he'd only been back in London for three days. "How are you feeling?" she queried when she realized she'd been staring at him.

"Better," he returned. The humor, though, left his eyes. "Why didn't you tell me about you and Simon?" he asked quietly.

She sobered as well, guilt flooding through her. "You've heard."

"I was bound to eventually, don't you think? Simon is my cousin, after all."

Angelique abruptly wanted to explain everything to him, to see the hurt and offended look leave his eyes. "I'm sorry," she returned. "I wanted to tell you, but—"

"But it is a secret, you know," another voice came from behind her.

"Simon!" she exclaimed, smiling as she turned around.

Simon swept a bow and stepped forward to kiss her knuckles. "I'm pleased you've returned from Paris." The glance over at his cousin was less than friendly. "I said we'd discuss this later, James. It is between you and me, and does not involve Angelique."

Angel rather thought that it did, but before she could protest, Brutus rose and walked over to Simon. He sniffed the boots of the son of Viscount Wansglen, then with a single half-hearted wag of his tail, returned to sit on Abbonley's foot. "Brutus, don't hurt the marquis," she reprimanded, tugging on the leash.

James grinned reluctantly. "It's all right. That's my good leg he's crushing." He glanced from her to Simon, then cleared his throat. "What do you think of this?" he asked, lifting the cane and twirling it once before he set it down again at Brutus's uncertain look. "Do I look dashing, or merely decrepit?"

Angelique laughed. "Oh, dashing, most definitely."

"Don't tell him that," Simon protested. "I've been trying to convince Jamie to stay in bed, and now you've told him he's dashing. There's nothing left to do but surrender."

"That's wise," James noted coolly. Apparently the marquis didn't like secrets, or at least ones he hadn't been let in on.

Simon grimaced at his cousin. "So that's your new pet, is it?" he queried, turning to eye the mastiff skeptically. "James said you'd acquired a dog. That, though, looks more like a pony."

"Hush, Simon," she chastised half seriously, "he's very

sensitive. He'll only eat if Henry or Helen or I sit with him.
I think he misses his companions.''

''Well, Angel, he's not exactly a house pet,'' Simon
pointed out.

Brutus licked his chops and sighed. ''He is now,'' Angelique returned, stepping over to pet the canine.

''Who are Henry and Helen?'' the marquis queried, looking down at her.

''My brother and sister,'' Angel explained, straightening.
''They're twins. Mama and Papa find them exasperating as
well.''

He grinned. ''Then I look forward to meeting them.''

After a moment spent smiling at him, Angel shook herself
and turned to Simon. ''That reminds me. I received a letter
from Lily yesterday. She expects to be in London late next
week.''

''That's wonderful. You've told me so much about Miss
Stanfred, I feel I already know her.'' Mr. Talbott glanced
over Angel's shoulder, his expression becoming more serious. ''But perhaps I could call on you for tea tomorrow, and
we can further discuss your friend's arrival.''

Angel turned to follow his gaze. Of the two dozen women
riding along the Ladies' Mile, all but a few seemed to find
the near end of the track much more interesting. ''Gossips,''
she scoffed, turning back again, disgusted at their transparent
curiosity.

''Gossips or no, it's not very seemly for us to be seen
standing here talking to you,'' her betrothed pointed out.

Angel looked over at Abbonley to find that he was watching her. Almost immediately he glanced away to look at their
audience, then turned back to Simon. ''Well, I've a mastiff
on my foot, so what do you suggest we do?''

Angel chuckled. ''Allow me. I hope.'' She tugged on the
leash. ''Come on, Brutus, there're some lovely rabbits for
you to chase just over here.''

With a heavy sigh the dog stood, looked at Simon, gave
another wag to James, and walked off. ''I'll see you tomorrow, Simon,'' Angel said over her shoulder.

"*Bon chance*, Lady Angelique." The marquis saluted her with the tip of his cane, and she grinned.

She knew the moment the two men were out of sight. Three of the riders ahead of her immediately dismounted and approached, while the others finally decided to try the other end of the track. "Angel, wasn't that the Marquis of Abbonley with Mr. Talbott?" one of them, her friend Jenny, queried.

"Yes, it was," she answered.

Louisa Delon looked distastefully at Brutus. "How do you know the Devil?"

"We arrived back in Dover at the same time. His coach hadn't arrived, so he rode home with us," Angelique answered, somewhat annoyed at Louisa's use of Abbonley's nickname.

"They say Gabriella Marietti was his mistress before he went off to war. Or one of them, anyway," Mary Hampston noted, unasked.

Angel glanced over at Mary. She had seen the famous opera singer on several occasions, and had thought her quite lovely. Now that she thought about it, though, there was something of a scratchy quality to the Italian woman's voice, so perhaps Miss Marietti wasn't as wonderful as everyone assumed. "Oh, was she?" she asked, trying to project just the right touch of boredom and disinterest into her voice.

Louisa and Mary glanced at one another. "The marquis is quite handsome," Louisa offered.

"Yes, he is," Angel agreed, thinking of those emerald eyes. The two gossips continued looking at her. "In an arrogant sort of way, I suppose," she added hurriedly. It wasn't very seemly for an engaged woman to be complimenting the looks, however handsome they might be, of her betrothed's cousin. Even if no one else knew she was engaged.

"So you were the first to know the Devil had returned to England," Mary commented.

"You shouldn't call him that," Jenny broke in. "What if he should return and hear you?"

"I wonder what Lady Kensington will think of his return," Louisa smirked.

Angel looked from one girl to the other, feeling as though she was missing something and not quite certain how to ask without sounding, well, like a gossip. "Desiree Kensington?" she finally asked weakly.

"Oh, yes, didn't you know?" Louisa went on, apparently happy to be imparting the information. "The Devil killed Viscount Luester over her."

"In a duel," Mary added unnecessarily.

Angel took a shaky breath. "Oh, my," she whispered. She knew there had been a duel and a scandal, but none of the details.

Mary nodded, twisting her reins in her gloved hands. "That was before she married Lord Kensington."

"Not by much," Louisa giggled, though she could only have been fourteen or fifteen at the time, for she was the same age as Angel. "They both wanted to marry her. During the duel the Devil waited until the viscount shot," she raised her hand as though holding a pistol and squinted down the imaginary barrel, "and then blew a hole right through his chest." She fired her finger at Brutus. Angelique flinched.

Mary shivered delicately. "That's why they call him the Devil."

"And that's not all he's done," Louisa continued, stepping forward. "Did you know three years ago he made a wager with Lord Renard about a race to Bath and nearly killed himself and Renard trying to beat him?"

"Did he win the bet?" Jenny asked.

"Oh, yes. Set a record, too. And there were rumors about him and Lord Renard's wife—"

"I apologize," Angelique broke in, "but I've a dressmaker's appointment. I'll see you all later, yes?"

They parted company, and thankfully Brutus was ready to return home as well. Angelique wished she had realized sooner about the duel. With the Devil back in London casting a pall over his family name, her parents would never agree to move the wedding date forward, much less publish an announcement. With her freedom so close to hand, the thought of waiting for nearly a year before achieving it was so frustrating she sometimes thought she would burst. She and Simon got along so smashingly, and in her own household she wouldn't have to follow the stifling, silly rules her mother and father seemed to have invented simply to cause her to be almost constantly in trouble. Angelique frowned. There had to be something that could be done.

She wanted to mention her concern to Simon, but at tea the next day and then at Almack's two days later she still hadn't been able to muster the nerve to say anything. After all, whatever the *ton* might think, the Marquis of Abbonley hadn't seemed all that scandalous to her. Instead, she found herself wondering why there was no sign of James Faring over the next few days, and how he must have felt upon learning that the woman he had killed for had married someone else.

The affair at the Sheffields the following Saturday was the first grand ball since her return to London, and it seemed as though the entire *haute ton* had turned out for it. "You look radiant," Simon greeted her as she joined the group of young people on one side of the huge, waxed dance floor. He took her hand and brushed her knuckles with his lips. "I have been waiting for nearly a month to dance with you."

She smiled. "You are so sweet to say that."

"Not at all. Has your Miss Stanfred arrived in town yet?"

Angel shook her head. "I'm expecting her any day now. I already wrote and asked her to be my bridesmaid, and—"

Simon laughed. "Angel, we do have nine months yet to plan this."

She shrugged. "I know, but it makes the wedding seem closer if I can do something to prepare for it."

"I know what you mean. In fact, I was thinking of asking James . . ." Simon trailed off, looking past her shoulder. At the same moment Angel noted that the room was buzzing with muted conversation.

"Lady Angelique."

She turned around. The Marquis of Abbonley stood before

her. He was dressed all in black, with only his white cravat and a beautiful emerald pin that exactly matched his eyes to leaven the stark effect. She suddenly realized why the nickname Devil had stuck to him.

"My lord," she answered, curtseying and wondering why he looked as though he was angry at her.

"I had hoped there would be a place left on your dance card for me," he murmured coolly, indicating with a flick of his long fingers the paper she held in one hand. "Under the circumstances, I thought perhaps we should become better acquainted."

She glanced down at her card. There were two spaces still unclaimed, but despite his completely legitimate reasoning, she debated whether or not to tell him. He seemed definitely put out about something, though she couldn't imagine what. Abbonley was watching her closely, no doubt expecting her to beg off.

"I have a waltz and a quadrille still unclaimed," she said, not one to back down from a challenge. "You may have your pick."

For a brief moment the look in his eyes changed, the only indication he gave that he might be surprised. "Then I choose the waltz," he replied, and with a slight bow made his exit.

With those words the music for the first quadrille of the evening began, and Simon led her out onto the floor. She glanced over toward the far wall to find the Marquis of Abbonley leaning there and watching her, and she wondered again what she had done. After a long moment she looked away to find Simon smiling at her from his place a few steps away, and she mentally shook herself. Whatever James Faring might think was certainly no concern of hers.

3

James Faring was not amused. The rumors of his supposed attraction to his cousin's lady had come to his ears the day after he had gone walking in Hyde Park. Simon's intended or not, the gossiping chit could have waited until the rest of the *ton* had a chance to decide for themselves if he had become civilized before she started in on what was left of his reputation. Behaving was difficult enough without that dragging him down.

In the past he would have spent the evening upstairs at the gaming tables, but he was avoiding those as strenuously as he was the liquor that flowed in abundance through the room. Most of his acquaintances, and even a few of his socially acceptable former mistresses, had stopped to greet him and welcome him home, but he wasn't much in the mood for frivolous conversation. He was saving all of his attention for Angel Graham.

By the time he claimed her for their waltz his leg ached, and he was nearly as tired as he was angry. For the first few turns they waltzed in silence, her slender hand tense in his as she obviously sensed his annoyance.

"No cane tonight?" she asked finally, raising her brown eyes to his.

"It was mostly for show," he returned shortly. "I should like to know, Lady Angelique," he said evenly, "how it has come to pass that half the wags in London are discussing my interest in the woman my cousin has been courting?''

She blanched. ''What?''

''You appear to be surprised.''

''I am.'' She frowned. ''Louisa and Mary only asked how we knew one another, and I said we'd returned to London together. I don't know where they got the idea that you were interested in me, or I, you. I should have known better than to say anything to those silly gossips with their odious innuendos.''

''Yes, you should have,'' he agreed.

Angelique glared at him, apparently not in any better humor than he was. ''I apologize, my lord, but surely you don't expect me to believe that you haven't had much worse said about you.''

''Rather blunt, aren't we tonight, my lady?'' he responded cynically. ''I shall be as well. Ordinarily I wouldn't give a flying leap what anyone might think about my actions, but I've been away for quite some time. I'd rather hoped to be able to redeem myself with my fellows.'' His voice sank into the murmur that, in the past, had caused several worthy gentlemen to give up frequenting White's while he was in town. ''You've now made things even more difficult for me. I do not appreciate that.''

''Then you likely shouldn't have accepted the offer of a ride back to London with us,'' she stated, her dark green skirts swirling against his legs.

He hadn't expected her to challenge him. Angelique Graham, though, didn't exactly seem the type to retreat. ''If you had informed me that you were engaged to my cousin, I might not have accepted that ride.''

Angelique glanced over at Simon, waltzing with Miss Jenny Smith. ''As he is your cousin, and as we have been engaged for three months, I thought he might have informed you already.'' She sniffed. ''And besides, when I invited you to share our coach, I had no idea who you were.''

He pursed his lips. Even her discovery of his identity had

had little discernable effect on her. "So we should be blaming Simon for this mess."

She shook her head. "My parents, I think. They're the ones trying to keep the engagement a secret." She grimaced. "They are obsessed with respectability, and are convinced I'll do something outrageous before the wedding and Simon will beg off."

"I see," he murmured, impressed and disarmed by her honesty. "Apparently then, you took quite a risk, inviting both Brutus and myself to join you." He paused as the rotation of the dance took them close to the line of bystanders and their sharp ears.

With the long evening, straying strands of Angelique Graham's copper hair, coiled into a bun at the back of her head, had come loose to caress her high cheekbones. The hint of a smile touched her full, red lips. "Actually, I thought that with a stranger sharing the coach ride, Mama wouldn't be able to rail at me as much for taking in another pet."

He raised an eyebrow, though where Angel was concerned, he had little difficulty imagining a version of the Dover rescue occurring on several other occasions. "Another pet?" he repeated.

"Well, there haven't been all that many, but Mama remembers every one, and all of the supposed problems they might have caused."

"I see," he returned with a grin. "So I was merely a distraction to keep your parents from realizing the true issue at hand."

She chuckled. "Exactly. Though I hadn't realized how much of a distraction you would be. A stranger would have done quite well, but the Devil—" Angelique stopped, flushing. "I'm sorry," she muttered.

"It's all right," he murmured, abruptly wondering how she would look with her long hair loose. He cleared his throat. "I worked quite hard to earn the epithet."

"So I've been hearing," she returned.

"Now you disapprove of me," he said, irked that her criticism bothered him. "I told you I've been attempting to reform."

"To use a cliché, talk, sir, is cheap."

"I begin to understand your parents' concerns, my lady." Two could play at insults, if that's what she wished.

Angelique flushed. "How dare you?"

"You see, my lady, I can be far more blunt than you."

She lifted her chin. "If this is how you become respectable, I can see why you're having such difficulty being accepted." Angelique glanced over at Simon. "Perhaps you need a wife to show you how to speak properly to a woman."

"Ah, a splendid idea. Perhaps you could find one for me."

That stopped her, as he had thought it might. "What?"

"A wife." He gave a goading smile. "Someone who would suit me and my needs."

She looked up at him suspiciously. Her eyes had small flecks of green deep inside them, he noticed. "What would suit you then, my lord?"

"Someone . . . mild, and respectable, from a good family," he responded slowly, though he found that that was not at all what he wished to say.

"Someone not like me, you mean," she scoffed.

"You are spoken for," he pointed out, wondering if Simon had any idea what a spitfire his future bride was.

"I am aware of that, sir." She cleared her throat. "What other qualities must this perfect wife possess, then?"

"I require nothing else."

"Sense of humor, intelligence, shared interests? Beauty?" she pursued, her expression becoming skeptical.

"Not necessary."

She hesitated. "Love?"

"There's no such thing," he returned bluntly, beginning to regret having brought up the matter, even in jest. She asked more questions than his grandmother.

"You don't believe that," she protested.

"How do you know what I believe, Lady Angelique?" he responded coolly. "I require a wife who will bear me an heir and stand beside me at social functions. I do not expect, nor do I require, anything further.''

The waltz ended. Angelique freed her hand from his grip, then after a moment wrapped her fingers around his forearm. She looked about the room with a frown. Abruptly, her expression cleared. ''Well then, my lord, allow me to assist you.''

''Why so suddenly cooperative, my lady?''

''You and I are to be cousins, after all,'' she returned. ''Your respectability will reflect on me.''

''I see.'' Exceedingly leery, James nevertheless allowed her to guide him to one side of the ballroom where several young women stood.

''Pearl?'' she said, and one of the girls turned around.

''Angel?'' the young lady replied, obviously surprised, then looked over at James and blushed.

''Pearl, may I present James Faring, the Marquis of Abbonley? My lord, Miss Pearl Wainwright.''

''My lord,'' the girl curtsied.

''Miss Wainwright,'' James acknowledged, looking sideways at Angelique. Miss Wainwright was blond and slim, and not at all unattractive, and he couldn't guess what Simon's chit might be up to. The music for a quadrille began, and he glanced back at the girl. ''Would you care to dance?''

''Yes, my lord,'' she responded, and took his proffered hand.

As Angelique watched them step into line with the other dancers, she barely refrained from laughing. If all James Faring required was a quiet, proper female, she would see that he found a plentitude. Then he would see whether affection or attraction had any importance in his match. No such thing as love, indeed.

''Angel,'' her mother motioned from the line of chairs set against one wall.

With a last glance at the couple, Angel stepped over to the countess. ''Yes, Mama?''

"You know your father and I disapprove of that man. Why do you insist on defying our wishes?"

"I wasn't defying you, Mama," Angel protested. "He asked me to dance."

"You should have declined."

"But once Simon and I are married, he will be my cousin. I can't—"

"You and Mr. Talbott will not be married for nine months. Once you are safely wed, then you may converse with the Marquis of Abbonley—as long as there is someone else present at all times. Even a married woman would find her reputation sullied in the presence of such a rake."

Despite her annoyance at him and the rumors he had informed her of, that didn't seem entirely fair. "But he told me he's trying to refor—"

"Angel, don't argue with me," Camellia returned. "For heaven's sake."

Fortunately, Simon approached Angel with a glass of punch in time to save her from the remainder of the tirade, and with a stiff nod the countess went to find her husband.

"Thank you," Angel said gratefully as she accepted the glass.

"You're welcome," he returned with a smile. "You looked as though you needed to be rescued."

She sent an exasperated look in her mother's direction. "She dislikes my even speaking with your cousin, as though he spits venom, or something."

"Some say he does." Simon grimaced and looked out toward the floor. "What in the world is he doing with Pearl Wainwright?"

"Dancing, I believe." She stifled another grin. "He requested an introduction."

"But Miss Wainwright is . . ." He trailed off, obviously unable to find a diplomatic way to say what he was thinking.

"Rather vacant?" she supplied. "And perhaps prone to the vapors?"

"Angel," Simon chided, glancing at the couple again. "Why didn't you tell him?" he whispered.

She shrugged, pursing her lips. "He didn't ask."

Other than Simon, Angel's visits to Naffley House were her favorite part of being engaged. She'd been taking tea with Simon's grandmother every Wednesday afternoon for the past three months, with the exception of the fortnight she'd been away in Paris. With Lady Elizabeth, as the dowager viscountess and daughter of the Duke of Newberry insisted on being called, she could speak her mind. Their conversations were often amusing and insightful, and now that she had met them both, Angelique was surprised at how much the older woman reminded her of the Marquis of Abbonley.

"Has Simon spoken to you about the estate in Warwickshire?" Lady Elizabeth asked, adding a spoonful of sugar to her tea.

Angelique nodded. "He mentioned that he thought he could persuade his father to let us set up a household there," she answered.

The viscountess pursed her lips. "Seems to me that stubborn son of mine should have offered it outright. Not as though he's set foot in it for the past five years."

Angelique was well aware that Lady Elizabeth was frequently frustrated by the stuffiness of her only son, Simon's father, the Viscount Wansglen. It was apparently her late daughter, James Faring's mother, who had been the more spirited of the two siblings. "Simon told me it's a lovely place," she offered with a smile.

The viscountess harumphed. "It's been in the Talbott family for generations," she noted. "An old stone and oak fortress that's stood against the Lancasters, floods, and the plague. It's something of a shrine. We all speak with bated breath about Turbin Hall."

That description varied somewhat from what Simon had told her. Living in an old fortress where every stick of furniture had its place and history sounded a bit . . . stifling. "It sounds enchanting," she responded firmly. Simon would certainly have no objection to her making some improvements on the manor once they were married.

Lady Elizabeth gave a cackle. "It sounds mouldy," she responded, "but you'll manage."

"Thank you, my lady."

Downstairs the door opened, followed by footsteps coming up the stairs. "Grandmama?"

"In here, Jamie," Lady Elizabeth called, giving a delighted smile.

James Faring pushed open the drawing room door. "Grandmama, I would appreciate it if you would stop trying to have me invited to every damned pheasant and fox hunt in the country this autumn," he snapped, limping into the room. His angry green eyes turned to Angelique, and he stopped in mid-stride. "My apologies, Lady Angelique," he said after a moment. "I didn't realize you were here."

"That's quite all right, my lord," Angel responded, noting that his long-fingered hands were crumpling someone's engraved calling card into an unrecognizable wad.

"I only asked if the Marquis of Westfall would be hosting his annual hunt," Lady Elizabeth commented, setting aside her tea, "and mentioned that you enjoyed hunting."

"You know bloody well that I do not enjoy—"

"Hunting with the Marquis of Westfall will do wonders for your reputation, my grandson."

He scowled. "Hunting with Westfall will give me an attack of apoplexy." Angel couldn't stifle a chuckle, and the marquis glanced over at her. "Do I amuse you?" he queried, raising an eyebrow.

She shook her head. "I'm trying to imagine you suffering from apoplexy."

He gave a slight grin. "Ah, but you've never seen me attempting to converse with Westfall."

The dowager viscountess snorted. "The last time you conversed with Westfall you relieved him of seven hundred pounds at Boodles' club, did you not?"

The marquis furrowed his brow. "Was that Westfall? I

remember it seemed quite amusing at the time, but—''

''What's amusing?''

Angel started. ''Simon,'' she exclaimed, as he strolled into the room.

He took her hand and raised it to his lips, then glanced over at his cousin. ''Generally, James, when someone is accompanying someone else, the first someone does not storm off in a rage and leave the second someone behind to make his apologies.''

''I didn't ask you to apologize,'' the marquis returned shortly. ''And if you and Grandmama would stop meddling in my affairs, I wouldn't have to go storming off anywhere.'' He glanced over at Elizabeth. ''Did it occur to either of you that I might simply want to spend this autumn at Abbonley? That I might enjoy being home after having been away for nearly two years?''

Lady Elizabeth stood. ''You're right, Jamie,'' she sighed, stepping over to kiss him on the cheek. She looked over at Angelique. ''May I leave you in the company of these rapscallions for a moment?''

''Of course,'' Angel agreed, glancing over at the marquis, and for the sake of her reputation grateful that Simon was present.

''What are you up to now, Grandmama?'' James queried suspiciously.

''I'm going to send a note to Julia Davern to inform her that I was in error and my grandson will not be available to go fox hunting after the Season.''

''Oh, good God,'' Abbonley groaned, motioning her out the door. ''Please.''

Simon grinned. ''You can't blame us for trying, you know.''

''Yes, I can.''

''I thought you wanted to be respectable,'' Angelique added, and was rewarded by a scowl from the marquis.

''That's correct, my lady. Respectable.'' He dropped onto the couch beside her. ''Not sent to Bedlam. That quadrille lasted for twenty-five minutes. I conversed, quite charmingly,

I might add, with Miss Wainwright for that entire time. I received three responses." He ticked them off on his fingers. " 'Yes, my lord,' 'no, my lord,' and 'whatever pleases you, my lord.' "

Angelique nodded and took another sip of tea. "That is what you required, is it not?" she said mildly. "I'm afraid I don't see the problem."

"What are you two talking about?" Simon interjected.

"That was bloody well *not* what I required," the marquis snapped, ignoring his cousin. His emerald eyes, though, seemed considerably less than annoyed as he met her gaze.

He was enjoying the argument, she realized. And so was she. "Miss Wainwright is quiet, respectable, and from a good family. That is what you—"

"All right. I see your point." James threw up his hands in mock surrender. "There's no need to stab me with it." He shook his head, a reluctant grin touching his lips. "Next time, please add intelligence to the list."

She nodded again. "Very well, my lord." Angel gave a slow smile she was unable to suppress. "I may have someone in mind for you." A brief, guilty thought crossed by her, but she ignored it. James Faring might truly wish for a wife, but she would show him that he couldn't simply pick a few choice ingredients and be happy with the results.

"Will someone *please* tell me what's going on?" Simon asked.

Before the conversation could continue, James's grandmother returned and Miss Graham had to take her leave. Elizabeth invited both of her grandsons to supper, then left them. With Angelique gone, the drawing room seemed quieter and darker, and James rose to go find something with which to occupy himself.

"James, may I speak to you for a moment?" Simon returned from the doorway where he had parted from his betrothed.

"That sounds rather formal," the marquis commented, nodding and sitting back again.

"You seem to . . . get along rather well with Angel."

That didn't sound promising. James raised an eyebrow. "That was an argument we were having, Simon."

"You like to argue," his cousin pointed out. "You always have."

"Well, excuse me for enjoying a spirited conversation. I thought you'd be happy that Lady Angelique and I are dealing well."

"I am. And stop being so hostile," Simon scowled, walking over to pour himself a brandy. He raised the decanter in James' direction. "Thirsty?"

The marquis shook his head. "No. And I'm not being hostile."

"You shouldn't be harassing Angel. It's bad enough that her parents are half ready to call off the wedding simply because the Devil's returned to London."

A muscle in the marquis' lean cheek twitched. "My apologies, cousin," he murmured, "if my having survived Waterloo is upsetting your wedding plans."

Simon flushed. "That's not what I meant."

"Well then, please, explain exactly what it is you did mean."

"James, I wanted . . . to ask your assistance."

"You've a funny way of going about it." He gestured in Simon's direction. "Continue."

"You know Angel and I don't want to wait until next April to marry," his cousin said slowly, and the marquis nodded.

"So I gathered."

Simon leaned back against the window sill. "Last night I happened to notice her mother's reaction to seeing the two of you waltzing."

"So you want me to stay away from her." The marquis stood, turning away so Simon wouldn't see how much that hurt. "Very well."

"No, James, I don't want you to stay away from Angel. Just the opposite, in fact."

Thinking he must have heard wrong, Abbonley stopped

halfway to the door and turned to stare at Simon. "What?"

"Her parents are concerned that perhaps we've rushed our decision to marry. What if they're right?"

James frowned, wondering why he hoped that what he was hearing was true. "Simon, it's certainly no concern of mine if you and Lady Angelique have changed—"

Shaking his head, Simon took a step forward. "What I mean is, what if the Marquis of Abbonley began showing interest in Angel? If they realized that, her parents would surely—"

James shook his head. "Absolutely not, Simon. I won't step between you and a woman. Ever. If I've learned one damned lesson, it's that one."

Simon paled. "It wouldn't be like . . . Desiree," he muttered. James turned again for the door, and Simon strode after him. "James, I'm sorry. I meant it would only be for show. It would only be to convince her parents that delaying the wedding would be a mistake." He lowered his hand. "That they'd be better off if they allowed us to wed immediately."

"No, Simon."

His cousin paused. "You owe me, James."

James turned to look at him. "I owe you?" he repeated slowly.

"I've spent most of my adult life helping you make your escape, literally and figuratively, out of women's bedchambers, making certain you returned home safely when you were too foxed to see straight and had just gambled some lord or other out of half his birthright, and," Simon hesitated for a moment, then raised his chin, "and being your second in duels."

He stopped, but James stood quietly, waiting for the rest. "And?" he finally prompted, looking at his cousin.

"And so I'm only asking one favor. A large one, I'll admit, but I'll never ask you for another."

"Why did you never write and tell me about your Angel?" James asked instead of answering.

Simon eyed him suspiciously, apparently sensing that he

was being put off. "It was actually something of a surprise."

"You mean you proposed by accident?" James returned, raising an eyebrow. "That seems a bit scatter-witted for you, cousin. You being the sensible one, and all."

His cousin relaxed a little. "It was no accident. I meant that we met early last Season, Angel and I, and we had so much in common and became such good friends, that, well, I suddenly realized I was very much in love with her."

James studied his cousin for a moment. "So elope."

Simon actually blanched. "I could never do such a thing. Angel's parents would never forgive us."

"But they'd forgive you playing this little game with their daughter's honor?"

"They won't know it's a game. And as the three of us will, her honor will never be at risk."

"What about the rest of the *ton*? They've already got their noses into this. And I'm trying to make amends. I'm looking for a wife. I don't want—"

His cousin snorted. "You? Looking for a wife?" He gestured toward the door Angelique had disappeared through. "That was what you two were talking about?"

"Why does everyone find the combination of myself and matrimony to be so damned amusing?" James growled.

Apparently seeing that he was serious, Simon sobered. "All right," he said, "find a wife. *After* you've helped me." He raised a hand when James began to protest. "Your reputation will receive barely another scuff. And with your wealth, there are females about who wouldn't care if you were a one-eyed dwarf with a hunched back, anyway."

"Simon—"

"James, please. I want to get married. Help me."

James sighed. "All right. But one of us is going to regret this." He looked over at his cousin, his expression serious. "And I hope it's me."

Simon stepped over and clasped his shoulder. "It will be neither of us. Trust me."

4

"When do I get to meet your Simon?" Lily Stanfred queried as she and Angelique rode together in Hyde Park.

"He's supposed to come for tea this afternoon," Angel smiled, then sighed.

"What is it?"

"Oh, just thinking. If I can stand my stuffy parents for another nine months, I'll be free."

"And then what?" Lily smiled.

Angelique threw out one hand. "I can do anything I wish! No one will complain about me ruining the floor or the furniture if I take in a stray dog, or cat, or ... fox; no one will tell me I'll be ruined if I want to go walking in my garden without my bonnet, or without my shoes; no one to disagree if I like the ratty old chair in the morning room and don't want it moved up to the attic."

"Heavens, Angel, it sounds as though you want to become a red Indian."

"Well, I don't wish to scalp anyone, of course," Angelique answered, then laughed. "I only mean that it will be pleasant to make decisions for myself, without someone else dictating what's best for me."

"As long as Simon approves," her friend pointed out.

"Oh, of course."

Angel smiled at Lily. If her friend had been there for the beginning of summer she might very easily have been named the toast of the Season. Fair-skinned, Lily Stanfred was gentle and elegant, with blue eyes soft as a lamb's and hair the color of—

"The pollen that peppers the petals of proud primroses," a voice lisped, and Angel looked up, startled.

Percival Alcott and his brother, Arthur, approached them. Angel cringed, for though she had managed to get through the Season with fewer than a dozen dances with both brothers, she considered even that number to be too many. "Beg pardon?"

"I said, my lady, that your exquisite companion's fair locks are the very color of the pollen that peppers the petals of proud primroses," Percival repeated, his slightly near-sighted gaze on Lily.

Angel gave her friend an amused glance. "Lily, may I present Mr. Percival and his brother, Mr. Arthur Alcott? Sirs, Lily Stanfred, daughter of Lord Stanfred."

"I'm pleased to meet you," Lily nodded somewhat uncertainly.

"Miss Stanfred," Arthur acknowledged. "A pleasure."

"I am a poet, you know," Percival stated, raising a monocle to gaze at Lily through one pale blue eye.

"I could tell immediately," Angel broke in, trying to stifle her laughter. She felt only a little guilt in her relief that Percival had set his sights on Lily rather than herself. Two more horsemen approached them, and the welcoming smile that came to her lips became even more amused as she recognized the second rider. Perhaps tonight she would have her chance to introduce Abbonley to his next possible intended.

"Angel," Simon Talbott greeted her as he reined in. "You look lovely, as always."

"Lady Angelique," James Faring echoed, giving her a speculative look when she was unable to cover her smile.

He was mounted on quite possibly the most splendid stallion she had ever seen, a coal black Arabian giant with a long mane and full, arched tail. She had forgotten that the marquis was as well known for his taste in horseflesh as he was for his scandalous reputation.

"I don't believe I've had the pleasure," the marquis said after a moment, looking over at Lily.

"Nor have I," Simon murmured, and kneed his bay gelding, Admiral, forward. "Forgive my boldness, but you must be Miss Lily Stanfred."

Lily smiled and placed her hand in Simon's waiting fingers. "Mr. Simon Talbott, I presume."

Smiling, Simon raised her hand to his lips. "None other. How was your journey to London?"

"Quite pleasant, Mr. Talbott. Thank you."

"Simon, please," Simon begged, and Lily nodded.

"Thank you, Simon."

"Don't mind the rest of us, Simon," the marquis said dryly.

Simon shook himself. "Beg pardon. James, Angel's dear friend Miss Lily Stanfred, and Mr. Percival Alcott and Mr. Arthur Alcott. Ma'am, gentlemen, James Faring, the Marquis of Abbonley."

"My lord," Percival said, twiddling his fingers in a bizarre version of a salute.

"I say, Abbonley, is it true you saved Wellington's life in Belgium?" Arthur asked, then subsided as it became apparent that he was being ignored.

Angel looked sideways at Abbonley to find him exchanging pleasantries with Lily, and she scowled, displeased. Her friend was no match for the Devil. And with him wife-hunting, there was no telling what might happen.

She was trying to decide how to intercede when a scrap of paper blew across the grass. At the sight of it her mare shied and reared. Used to the gray's flightiness, she leaned forward and pulled on the reins. Before she could complete the action a hand grabbed her bridle and hauled the mare down.

"Let go! I can manage," she snapped, looking up to see the marquis close enough to touch, his eyes on her.

He obliged, releasing his grip, but didn't move away. "So I see. You sit well, my lady."

Before she could respond, Percival decided it time to put his twopence in. "That mare is too unpredictable for a lady," he noted stuffily.

"Lady Angelique handles her well enough," the marquis contradicted.

"Heaven is not unpredictable," she argued, glaring at Percival. "She's spirited, not a half-dead cart mule like you ride."

"Angel," Simon admonished.

The marquis gave a shout of laughter, his eyes dancing as he met her irritated gaze. She had already begun trying to decide how to take back what she had said, but as she looked at the amused expression on his handsome face the notion, and her annoyance, faded.

"Heaven?" he chuckled, raising an eyebrow.

Percival, blustering at the insult to his mount, bobbed his head. "Again, highly improper."

"What do you call your . . . steed?" the marquis asked.

Percival flushed. "Lancelot," he said loftily.

"Ah, a noble moniker, indeed."

Angel was enjoying the exchange. Anyone who thought Percival Alcott as great a fop as she, and had the wherewithal to point it out, was definitely an ally.

"And what do you call that?" Alcott asked, indicating the marquis's grand stallion.

"Demon," Abbonley answered promptly.

Angelique chuckled, then stopped as both men looked her way. One gaze was pale blue and patronizing, the other wickedly amused emerald. She cleared her throat, seeing her chance. "There is to be a recital tonight at the Countess of Beaufort's. Lily and her mother will be going with Mama and me." She turned to look at Simon. "Will you both be attending?"

Simon threw a quick glance at the marquis, who shrugged. "It sounds quite tolerable. Why not?"

Angel smiled. "Why not, indeed?"

The rest of the day seemed interminably long, and even after she arrived at the Countess of Beaufort's drawing room with her mother, Lily, and Lady Stanfred, she was hard-pressed to keep from pacing. Most of the guests had arrived and were milling about the entrance to the music room, but Simon and the marquis had yet to appear. Since Abbonley was the only reason she'd suggested they all attend, she was beginning to feel quite aggravated.

Finally the two gentlemen appeared at the top of the stairs. The unexpected presence of the marquis immediately set the rest of the guests, most of them female, buzzing. As soon as she spied Abbonley, the Countess of Beaufort parted from Lady Andrews and elbowed her way through the crowd to greet him. It took the two gentlemen several minutes to make their way over to Angelique's party, and she smiled, mostly with relief, as Simon reached her side.

"Angel," he greeted her, brushing her knuckles with his lips. "And Miss Stanfred," he smiled, repeating the gesture. "Good evening, ladies."

"I had no idea these functions were so popular," the marquis commented, taking her hand in turn.

"The countess serves exceedingly savory refreshments," Angel explained, *sotto voce,* and he chuckled.

"So that's the secret. I thought it might be the music."

Angelique glanced across the room to see that the other guest she had been waiting for had also arrived. "Mama," she said, "Excuse me for a moment. Lord Abbonley has asked me to introduce him to someone."

Camellia Graham stifled a frown. "The recital is due to start any moment, darling, so please hurry," she agreed reluctantly.

The marquis was eyeing her curiously, but followed her willingly enough. "My future bride?" he queried at a whisper.

"She meets all of your requirements," Angel returned. "Miss Peachley?"

The tall young woman, leaning against one wall and looking quite bored, turned her head. "Yes, Lady Angelique?"

the brunette answered, fingering her fashionable cropped ringlets.

"May I present James Faring, the Marquis of Abbonley? My lord, Miss Hester Peachley."

"Miss Peachley," Abbonley said pleasantly, reaching for her fingers in his usual bold manner.

Miss Peachley turned her wrist to shake his hand instead. "Abbonley," she returned. "I didn't know you attended recitals."

"Oh, I always enjoy something new," he offered, giving Angelique a suspicious glance. "Your name sounds somewhat familiar to me."

"Yes? Perhaps you've read one of my articles. I am a supporter of women's liberation."

"Ah," he murmured. "Liberation from what, if I may ask?"

"Men."

"From the subjugation of men, or from the presence of the male of the species?" James queried pleasantly. His lips twitched, and Angelique thought he must be amused. She stifled a smile.

"Men have used women as nothing more than procreative slaves for far too long. It is my belief that this must—"

"Angel, we're going in," her mother hissed, pulling at her arm.

"Excuse me," Angelique muttered, reluctantly turning away.

They found themselves in the back row. Simon had seated himself next to Lily's mother, and the three of them were discussing the Stanfred estate, only a mile or so from Niston. In a moment they had pulled her mother into the discussion as well. Finally, Miss Charlotte Hartford took a seat at the pianoforte and began to play, and the room quieted down.

Several minutes into the piece someone took a seat beside Angelique, but she was trying to remember which of Mozart's pieces was being suffocated, and didn't pay any attention until she felt her fingers gripped. Startled, she glanced over to see the marquis looking sideways at her. Quickly she faced front again.

"What are you doing?" she whispered.

After a hesitation his fingers released hers. "Hester Peachley is a damned blue-stocking," he murmured back, "you little hoyden."

"What's wrong with being well-read?" she protested, surprised he had lasted for as long as he had. Generally, Miss Peachley wiped out her male companions in less than a minute.

He gave a slight shake of his head. "There is absolutely nothing wrong with either a well-read woman or the ability to converse in an intelligent and insightful manner."

"So what is the difficulty?" she returned, hiding a grin and not at all surprised to hear that he was so enlightened.

"The difficulty is that a blue-stocking wields her knowledge like a damned battle axe, cutting down every male opponent within earshot."

"You were wounded then?"

"Nearly mortally."

Laughter burst from Angelique's lips, and she quickly raised her hand to smother it. Her mother and the ladies directly in front of her turned to glare. Those two women began whispering to their companions, and only a moment later it seemed everyone in the room had turned to see that the Marquis of Abbonley was seated beside her. "Go away," she murmured at him through clenched teeth.

"But we are nearly cousins," he protested.

"I thought this is what you were complaining about before. And no one knows Simon and I are engaged. You'll ruin everything." Finally everyone's attention returned to the front of the room as Miss Hartford's playing became more enthusiastic. "Go away," she repeated. "I introduced you to Miss Peachley because she's respectable and from a good family and intelligent, just as you wanted. Go converse with her."

"Not for a hundred pounds," he returned indignantly, and she had to stifle another laugh.

"You'll make Simon angry," she warned.

Abbonley leaned forward to look across her. His skin smelled faintly of shaving soap. Angel licked abruptly dry lips and reluctantly turned to follow his gaze. "Simon appears to be quite content," he commented. It did look that way, but then Simon loved classical music. "Besides, I'd rather converse with you."

With a blush she determinedly faced front again. "I'm not speaking to you," she whispered, though his comment quite pleased her. "I'm listening to Mozart."

He leaned closer. "It's Haydn," he murmured, his breath soft in her ear, and she shivered.

"Shh," she muttered, swallowing. "I hate these stuffy things anyway."

"Then why are you here?" He paused for a moment, then out of the corner of her eye she saw him grin. "To introduce me to Miss Peachley, of course. I appreciate the sacrifice."

"Quiet," she admonished when her mother glanced hostilely at the two of them.

"And speaking of classic creations," he went on, undaunted, "how is your Brutus?"

Actually she was worried about the mastiff, but extending this conversation further would be perilous to her reputation, and her equilibrium. James Faring, she was finding, could be quite unsettling. "He's tolerable," she returned.

"Perhaps I shall come visit him," the marquis commented. Before she could reply the piece ended, and he joined in the applause.

5

"I did try to warn you that Miss Peachley can be rather . . . biting," Simon said as he and James sat at the breakfast table the next morning.

"You told me that already. Yes, I know. I should pay attention to you. Pass the marmalade."

Simon passed the bowl. "Then why did you go back to talk to her at intermission?"

"Because she irritated me excessively."

"You gave her a set down, didn't you?"

James grinned and motioned for the plate of bacon. "Me? What gave you such an outlandish idea as that?"

Simon laughed, then leaned back and eyed his cousin. "You are in a good mood today," he commented.

James grunted noncommittally. In truth he was in a good mood. He had concocted a plan last night before retiring, and the smile it brought to his lips had developed a tendency to return when he didn't expect it.

"Hm. Do you go to Gentleman Jackson's with me today, then?" Simon asked, apparently realizing he wasn't going to get a further explanation.

James grimaced and flexed his shoulder. "Don't believe I'm up to boxing yet," he said ruefully, wondering if he would ever be able to do so much as dress again without flinching. "You are eventually going to let Lady Angelique

45

in on your plan, aren't you?'' he queried offhandedly, rising.

Simon gave a short smile. ''I told her last night, after the recital.''

''And?''

''She—how did she put it—thought it was delightfully silly of me, I believe.''

''It is rather out of character, cousin,'' James noted, disappointed. He had actually been hoping to hear what Angelique's reaction to his flirting had been.

His cousin grimaced. ''I know. I hope her parents never find out the truth.''

''Do you wish to give up your scheme, then?'' James queried. Abruptly, he hoped his rather stiff cousin wouldn't back down. Teasing with Angelique, a farce or not, was the most amusement he'd had since before he'd gone off to France with Wellington.

Simon shrugged. ''No. Angel would be heartbroken. She already complains that I'm too conventional.''

''Good for her,'' the marquis applauded. ''You never listened to me when I complained about your propensity for propriety.''

''Very amusing, Jamie.''

James grinned and headed for the door. ''I'll see you at lunch.''

He had already arranged to have Demon saddled and waiting for him, and in a short time found himself in a section of London he rarely frequented. His task accomplished and the well-wrapped parcel in hand, he headed back to Mayfair, a grin once more on his face as he reached the Grahams' house. Belatedly he realized he should have informed Simon of his intentions, but this was all his cousin's idea, anyway. Besides, he wanted to hear from Angelique what she thought of this absurd little scheme.

At his knock the door was opened by a white-haired butler, who almost managed to mask his surprise at the unexpected visitor. ''If you will wait here a moment, my lord,'' the butler said, ushering him into the hall and walking through a door, James's calling card in his hand.

"Give Millicent back!"

A small form hurtled down the stairs and slammed into James before he could dodge out of the way. He took the impact with a grunt and reflexively put out a hand to steady the small person stepping back away from him. It was a boy of perhaps nine years, the red-brown hair and brown eyes immediately identifying him as a Graham.

"Apologies, sir," the boy said. A look of wonderment came over his face. "You're the Marquis of Abbonley, ain't you?"

"Give me Millicent, you beast!"

A second form came down the stairs, showing little more decorum than the first. This time James was ready, and he sidestepped to avoid a collision. The slim, bright-eyed girl gave him an insight as to what Angelique must have looked like as a child.

"Hullo," she said, then lunged for the boy. "Give her back, Henry!"

The boy had a doll in one hand, his fist wound through the poor thing's hair, though it looked as if such rough treatment could do little more damage than had already been inflicted. "Not until you give me Hero back!" he returned at equal volume, dodging behind James.

"I don't have your stupid horse. You lost it!"

"Did not!"

"Did too!"

The marquis was beginning to feel like a maypole. "Where was Hero last seen?" he queried.

Henry stopped, and the girl wrenched the doll out of his hand. "That's not fair, Helen," he snapped.

"You stopped," she retorted.

"But he's the Marquis of Abbonley," Henry protested, gesturing at James. "He was wounded in the war, and he's a member of the Four-Horse Club." He bounced on his toes. "Drives to an inch, they say."

"And you must be Henry," James commented, amused.

The boy drew himself up straighter. "Yes, sir. Henry Graham, my lord." He eyed the girl. "And this is my sister, Helen."

"How come you to know so much about me, Henry?"

"Henry knows everything about members of the Four-Horse Club," Helen supplied, holding the doll in the same manner that her brother had.

"I'm flattered," he said, holding out his hand. Henry shook it vigorously.

"Henry, Helen, don't harass our guest."

Lady Niston stepped into the hallway to herd her young ones away. Angelique stood behind her in the doorway, chuckling. Henry dodged around his mother and headed back for James.

"Did you drive here in a rig?" he asked.

James returned his attention from Angel. "Rode my horse."

"What's his name?" Helen asked from under her mother's arm.

"Demon."

"I say," Henry exclaimed. "He's the black Arabian you rode from London to Bath in thirty-eight hours, ain't he?"

James nodded, surprised the boy knew of that, though it was one of his few repeatable exploits. "He is."

"Oh, may I see him? Please? Please, Mama? They set a record!"

"My lord?" she queried, grabbing Helen by her skirt and apparently accustomed to the pair's high spirits. She would have to be, if her older daughter was any indication.

He smiled. "Just don't touch him," he warned, and the two headed for the door. "He bites."

"Yes, my lord. We'll be careful," Henry called over his shoulder.

"I'd best go see to that." Lady Niston sighed, then hesitated. "Pimroy," she said, turning to the butler and gesturing at the wall, "please straighten those paintings again." With another displeased glance at James she excused herself to follow the children.

"Lady Angelique," James said, taking Angelique's hand, "we seem to be nearly alone."

"Which is to say we are not, my lord," she responded with a grin, pulling her fingers free. "And Simon told me all about his plan, you know." She gave him a scowl. "You might have let me in on it sooner."

James raised his hands in surrender. "I am only the loyal vassal. Blame your betrothed for keeping you in the blind about this."

She grimaced. "All right." With a glance at the butler she sighed. "I have to admit, hearing the truth from him did leave me somewhat relieved. Last night you were very : . . " she flushed, "charming."

"You mean to say you thought my attentions sincere?" he queried softly, enchanted. She looked up at him, and after a long moment he dropped his eyes from hers. This wasn't a seduction, for Lucifer's sake. There were no witnesses but the butler for him to impress with his interest in the chit. "You were flattered, I hope."

She grinned ruefully. "A bit flustered, actually."

Trying to ignore the fact that her admission had pleased him greatly, James retrieved the package he had procured earlier and held it out to her. "I wanted to thank you," he said, "for assisting me in my search."

Angelique's eyes snapped to his face. "You mean you've found someone?"

"Not yet," he smiled, not surprised at her displeasure. No doubt she had several other eccentric females yet to foist on him. He looked forward to meeting them. "I remain hopeful, however."

With a grin, she opened the box. Angelique gave him a delighted look as she uncovered the contents, then broke into a gale of laughter that he found quite engaging and returned with a chuckle of his own. She lifted her prize for closer examination.

"Oh, it's perfect," she managed, holding it up to the light.

"I did try," he answered. It was quite possibly the most splendid dog collar he had ever set eyes on, with a dozen multi-hued stones set into a thick leather collar. The shop-keeper had looked stunned when the Devil had entered her curio shop, and even more so when he had gone directly to the thing and asked the woman to wrap it up, because he would be taking it with him. "I thought it might perk him up," he commented, reaching out to polish one of the *faux* gems with his cuff.

"I don't know about Brutus," she exclaimed, laughing harder, "but I adore it."

James smiled. "Then I am content," he said softly.

"Are you?" She blushed prettily, then raised her long-lashed gaze to his. He was seized by a desire to kiss her so compelling that he took a step forward before he could stop himself.

James froze, horrified and dismayed at his reaction to her. If there was one woman on the face of the earth that he had no right to even think of kissing, it was Angelique Graham. She was Simon's, for God's sake.

The front door opened, and he jumped. Henry charged in, running circles around his father, while Helen and Lady Niston walked behind them. "Oh, Papa, I want a grand horse like that. I shall name him Devil, or perhaps Lucifer. May I?"

"Certainly not," his mother countered sternly.

Lord Niston nodded as he saw them. "James," he said, shaking Abbonley's hand. "Splendid animal."

James took a breath, trying to gather his thoughts. "Thank you, Niston. You have a splendid family."

With a woof Brutus bounded through the doorway. "Brutus, no!" Angelique ordered. The dog skidded to a halt at James's feet and demanded to be petted. James complied, grateful that for once the mastiff hadn't chosen to sit on him.

"I say, my lord marquis, have you let Demon stand at stud yet? Could I have one of the foals?" Henry asked.

Beside him Angelique chuckled. "I have, and no, I don't believe any are available at the moment," he answered with a grin. "You ride then, Master Henry?"

"Oh, yes. Only my Ajax is slow, and he won't jump."

"And Papa won't get him another," Helen supplied, coming forward to look at what her sister held. "What's that? It's ugly."

Angel lifted the collar and grinned. "It's a gift from the marquis." She leaned over and showed it to Brutus, who apparently approved of it enough to give the collar and her hand a wet lick. That in itself would have been enough to cause some proper females to lose their composure, but Angelique only smiled and fastened the jeweled band around the mastiff's neck.

"If it's from the marquis, then it ain't ugly," Henry said firmly, though he eyed it dubiously.

"It is," Helen retorted defiantly.

"It ain't!"

"My lord, I must apologize for these hooligans," Niston grimaced.

James smiled. "No need. I've been told I'm quite the hooligan myself." He nodded, noting that Angel was smiling at him. The grandfather clock on the landing chimed twelve, and he shook himself. "Please excuse me. I promised Simon I'd go with him to one of his stuffy clubs for some luncheon."

"It was splendid to meet you, my lord," Henry enthused, offering his hand.

"And you, as well." James reached down and shook it solemnly, then winked at young Helen. "Good day, and thank you again, Lady Angelique," he intoned with a grin. "I am grateful to you."

He lasted only twenty minutes in Simon's club before the dull and pointless conversation the other members were earnestly engaged in drove him to leave and head for White's, where at least he could get a meal without being made to fall asleep. When he had decided to become respectable, he hadn't realized that being so frequently bored would accompany it.

His reputation did earn him a prime spot at the horse auctions the next morning, though Simon saw fit to point out that it was because of the size of his purse and not of his temper. "Forgive me if I'm not terribly flattered by that," James commented offhandedly, eyeing his information sheet and the matched pair of coach horses being paraded about the yard before him while the auctioneer sorted out the noisy bids of his fellows.

"You like them?" Simon queried, resting his arms along the corral railing.

"No," he answered, looking across the yard. The sight of a young boy and girl perched up on the railing there caught his attention, and he straightened, trying to see behind them. "Short-chested. No wind."

"You think so?"

"Mm-hm." The two youngsters had been joined by their father and their lovely older sister. Angelique was in a pretty green muslin that brought out her hair's copper highlights, and she seemed to be using her parasol to bat at her bois-terous brother rather than to shade her face. The auction was an unusual place to find a young woman of quality, but then a great many things about this particular lady seemed to be out of the ordinary. Henry gestured excitedly at the next an-imal brought out, but after a moment Angelique shook her head and frowned, saying something to her father.

"This one?" Simon asked, looking over at him.

"Hm? Oh. Weak left foreleg," James murmured absently. "Probably been kicked."

His cousin pursed his lips. "Speaking of being kicked," he ventured, "why isn't Grandmama assisting you in your search for a wife? I would think that would be more fitting."

"She's refused to aid me. And my next closest female relative would appear to be either your mother—"

"Oh," Simon grimaced.

"Or your betrothed. Besides, Lady Angelique rather volun—"

"The engagement is a secret, remember?" Simon glanced at the crowd around them, but no one appeared to be paying attention to their conversation. "It's just that I'm not convinced Angel's choices would be suitable for what you want in a wife.''

James raised an eyebrow, feigning surprise. ''And why do you say that?''

His cousin shrugged. ''Well, she can be rather . . . whimsical, sometimes.''

''Really? I hadn't noticed.''

''Yes, really. And do keep in mind that your search for love is to wait until after you've finished helping us.''

''For a wife,'' James corrected sharply. ''Not love.''

The look Simon gave him wasn't at all the expression one should be wearing when discussing matrimony, and James suspected he was about to be lectured. ''It's been almost five years,'' Simon muttered predictably. ''Stop torturing yourself. You're allowed to fall—''

''In love again?'' James finished for him. ''How do you know that, Simon? How long is one expected to do penance for a murder?''

''It wasn't a murder. It was a fair fight, James.''

''Tell that to Luey.''

For a moment Simon looked at him, then shook his head and stepped back from the railing. ''I know you'd take it back if you could. Perhaps Luester realizes that as well.'' He sighed when James declined to respond. ''You said you'd go to tea at Grandmama Elizabeth's at three. Don't be late.'' His cousin turned and walked away.

''Tea,'' James grumbled. ''How very conventional of me.''

He glanced up to see Angelique looking at him, a smile on her face. With her parasol blocking her from her father's view, she motioned him over. After a moment James took a breath and nodded back, tilting his beaver hat at her. Belatedly he wondered if he shouldn't have informed Simon that his betrothed was in attendance. He shrugged. His cousin should have noticed her, himself.

He pushed away from the fence to make his way through the crowd to the Grahams. ''Good day, Niston,'' he smiled. ''Lady Angelique, little Grahams.''

Helen giggled, but Henry leaned down from his perch on the railing and tapped James on the shoulder. "My lord marquis?"

James reluctantly looked away from Angelique and over at her brother. "Yes?"

"Have you bid on anything yet?"

He shook his head. "No, but I'm about to."

"On what?"

"That one." He pointed at the magnificent bay being led out and held his information sheet so Henry could see it.

"Pharaoh," the boy read, and looked over at the stallion again. "He's a goer, ain't he?" he said admiringly.

"Oh, my," Angel murmured, resting her chin on her arms and sighing as she leaned up against the railing. "He's splendid."

James found that he was somewhat distracted. "Perhaps you can ride him some day."

She turned her head to look up at him. "You don't own him yet," she pointed out.

"I will."

"That is the greatest piece of nonsense I have yet heard this Season," she said with a grin.

James chuckled. "And what might the second greatest piece of nonsense be, my future cousin?" he murmured, raising an eyebrow.

"Anything Percival Alcott says," she returned promptly.

James put a hand to his heart. "I don't know whether to be flattered or offended by my place in the ranking."

"My lord?" Henry queried from his other side.

Angelique wrinkled her nose. "You're correct. Percival Alcott is a much greater piece of nonsense. I apologize."

"My lord," Henry protested, pulling on his sleeve, "they're bidding!"

James shook himself and turned around. With a grin he handed the rolled information sheet over to Henry. "Wave this in the air when I tell you," he instructed.

"Yes, sir!"

The auctioneer called out a hundred pounds, already a

steep price, and he nodded. Henry obediently waved the paper in the air, and James raised a hand.

"One hundred to the Marquis of Abbonley," the auctioneer droned. "Do I hear one twenty-five?"

"One twenty-five," came from across the paddock.

"Uh-oh," Angel muttered. "The fifth Earl of Branford wants your hunter."

"Well, he can't have him," James returned, and nodded at Henry.

"One hundred fifty to the Marquis of Abbonley. Do I hear one hundred seventy-five?"

"Two hundred," Branford bellowed.

"Three," James murmured before the auctioneer could repeat the amount.

Henry craned himself up to his full height. "Three hundred!" he shouted.

The crowd quieted to an expectant murmur. "Three hundred fifty," the earl called out, eyeing James with some hostility.

"Four," James returned, and Henry seconded it at greater volume.

"That's quite high, don't you think?" Angel murmured, her sleeve brushing against his.

"I want him," James responded softly.

"You want him, or you don't want Branford to have him?" she returned.

He glanced over at her. "It's the same thing."

"My lord marquis, the bidding stands at four hundred fifty pounds," the auctioneer informed him. "Do you have another bid?"

He nodded. "Let's get this over with. Henry? One thousand pounds."

Henry grinned. "One thousand pounds!" he yelled into the silence.

The auctioneer was stunned enough that he delayed a moment before responding. "One thousand pounds from the Marquis of Abbonley. Are there any other bids?"

Branford glared at James for a moment, then shook his

head. "You can have the nag," he called, and turned away.

"Thank you," James returned, and as the auctioneer slammed his mallet onto the crate in front of him the crowd exploded into cheers and applause.

"Sold, Pharaoh, to the Marquis of Abbonley, for one thousand pounds." The auctioneer sketched a deep bow. "Thank *you*, my lord."

James grinned and raised his hat. "I'd best go pay for my nag."

"Can we go?" Henry asked, jumping down from the fence.

"All right," Niston sighed, and lifted Helen to the ground.

"One thousand pounds?" Angel repeated, falling into step beside James.

He smiled and leaned closer. Other members of the *ton* had noted his companion and were muttering among themselves. The engagement might be a secret, but everyone knew Simon Talbott was courting Angel Graham. It was an annoyance, but his name could take the additional scuffing Simon had envisioned. He did wonder, though, if his cousin had realized that Lady Angelique's reputation might be at risk. "Haven't I told you I'm fabulously wealthy?"

She grinned at him. "Not for long, if you keep this up."

"Would you rather I spent it on you?"

Angelique glanced over at her father and the twins. "I haven't asked you for anything, my lord," she replied, lifting her chin.

"Why don't you?" he challenged. "Ask me for anything." He was abruptly surprised to realize he would happily grant any request she might have. "A wedding present, perhaps? Might I recommend real jewels to match the *faux* ones I purchased for Brutus?"

She looked over at him. "Five pennies," she said after a moment.

"Beg pardon?" he queried, not expecting her to answer at all. A lady wasn't supposed to acknowledge even the offer of a gift from a rake such as himself, yet she'd already accepted the mastiff's collar. Perhaps she wasn't aware of the convention.

Angelique held out her hand. "Five pennies, if you please."

Grinning and again baffled by what she might do next, James reached into his pocket and handed her the coins.

"Thank you," she smiled, hazel eyes twinkling, and with a flick of her skirts took Helen's hand to lead her sister over to a confectioner selling strawberry ices.

James looked after her, chuckling, until Niston stepped up and blocked his view. "That's a fine animal," he said stiffly. "Will you keep him in town?"

James shook his head. "No. I'll take him with me to Abbonley when I return."

"So you will be leaving London soon?"

That was hardly subtle, but not unexpected. Annoying the parents with his attentions to the daughter was the plan, after all. "I should be getting back," he agreed, then deliberately glanced over at Angelique. "But I've decided to stay in town through the end of the Season."

He left his note with the auctioneer's assistant and received the tether of the hunter. "Do you approve my purchase?" he asked Henry.

"Oh, yes," the boy gushed. Abruptly he sobered. "And I still have old Ajax," he said dejectedly, and kicked at a clod of dirt.

James smiled, unexpectedly remembering a stodgy old pony he'd had in his youth. "You know, Master Henry, I may have a steed that would suit your needs in my stables at Abbonley."

"You do?" Henry whispered, brown eyes going round.

James nodded. "I believe so." He glanced again at Angel and took a breath. "And I would be pleased to invite your family to come holiday with me after the Season. Perhaps a belated engagement party for Lady Angelique and my cousin?"

"Oh, Papa, could we? Please, could we? Oh, to ride a horse from the Marquis of Abbonley's stables. Please?"

Angelique was watching him, her green parasol dragging in the dirt and her eyes sparkling in the sunlight. "It would be my pleasure," he cajoled.

"Please, Papa?" both twins pleaded in unison.

The earl glanced for a moment at his daughter as well, then frowned. "There is officially no engagement," he returned shortly, "so there is no need for a party. And I have business at Niston. Thank you for your invitation, my lord, but I must refuse."

James inclined his head, hiding his anger at the insult in a smile. "Of course. I understand," he returned. When he glanced at Angel she appeared disappointed, but then they'd just missed out on a fine opportunity to raise Simon in her parents' eyes by showing the Devil off in his own scandalous element at Abbonley. He was disappointed as well, but for a different set of reasons entirely.

6

Angelique rose late, having spent a restless night with horses, splendidly garish dog collars, and emerald eyes haunting her sleep. That last bit was odd, for Simon's eyes were blue.

She and some friends were to go picnicking at midmorning, and Tess helped her into her peach-colored sprig muslin before she and Brutus hurried downstairs. "Good morning, Angel," her mother smiled, motioning her to take a seat at the breakfast table.

"I can't," she replied, kissing each of her parents on the cheek. "Simon will be here at any moment." She dipped her forefinger into a bowl of strawberry jam and lifted it to her lips.

"You certain you don't want a piece of toast to go with that?" her father asked, pausing with his teacup halfway to his mouth.

She licked the sweet, sticky jam off her finger, then accepted the napkin he held out. "If I can't have bad manners here, where can I have them?"

"Nowhere," her mother answered.

"Oh, that reminds me," Angel said, seeing a chance to aid their cause. "The Marquis of Abbonley has invited us to share his box at the opera Thursday night. *Don Giovanni.* He said he wanted to become better acquainted with us, since we're to be part of the family. It will be splendid, don't you think?''

"Angel," her father began, frowning, as Pimroy pulled open the front door.

"I mustn't be late," she said with a smile.

"That dog is not going with you," her mother stated.

"Oh, Mama," Angel grumbled. "All right. Brutus, stay."

The dog sighed and padded upstairs to find the twins, as Simon entered the hall and took her hand. She hoped there was no jam left on her finger.

"Good morning," she smiled, grateful that she and Lily had overheard what was being performed at the opera. All that remained was to get word to the marquis that they were to go.

It was an easier task than she expected. Shortly after they arrived at St. James Park they were joined by Lily, Louisa and Mary, the Alcotts, and Richard Forbes and his cousin, Sophia. As they all sat on the spread of blankets they were approached by a rider on a magnificent black stallion.

"Good day," the marquis said, leaning down to shake Simon's hand as his cousin rose to greet him. "I didn't expect to find all of you here."

His glance at Simon was less than pleased, and as he dismounted Angel wondered if his cousin hadn't tricked Abbonley into joining them. He glanced about the group, inclining his head at Lily and giving a slight nod to the Alcotts. As his gaze found Angel, he gave a smile and stepped forward to bend over her raised hand. "Lady Angelique," he greeted her.

"James, do you stay?" Simon asked, apparently sensing his cousin's misgivings at the rather dull composition of the gathering. If not for Simon and Lily, Angel would have been looking for a way out, herself.

The marquis shook his head. "I have an appoint—"

Fearing he would leave before she had a chance to speak to him, Angelique hammered her fist against the ankle of his boot.

"—ment with my secretary, but I believe I have a few

moments," Abbonley finished smoothly. His limp more pronounced than it had been a moment earlier, he seated himself
beside her. "Why do you insist on bashing me, my lady?"
he murmured, accepting a glass of madeira from Mr. Forbes.

"We need to talk," she returned, noting that he set the
glass aside without drinking. That surprised her, for with his
reputation she had expected him to down it at one go and
ask for another.

"I'm listening."

"I told my parents you'd invited us to share your box at
the opera on Thursday," she continued, ignoring the others
as Louisa Delon began one of her tiresome *on dits* about
someone or other's scandalous behavior.

He squinted one eye. "That was bold of me," he commented, "considering I don't have a box at the opera."

She hadn't thought of that. "But—"

"My grandmother does, however," he interrupted with a
short grin. "I believe I can persuade her to have us all there
on Thursday." He handed her half of his peach.

"I hope so," Angel muttered. "If we can't accomplish
something before the Season ends and we go our separate
ways, my parents will have no reason to change any plans
at all." She grinned. "That was a grand idea you had, to
invite us to Abbonley. I suppose Simon's plan is working a
bit too well, and Papa didn't want me around you." She
glanced over at Simon, who was laughing as he refilled
Lily's glass.

The marquis smiled, lifting his glass of madeira and eyeing the liquid before he set it down again. "And the Season's
not over yet, Lady Angelique."

"All right, Jamie, what's on your mind?"

James selected another card from the pile, grimaced, and
discarded it. "Beg pardon?" he queried, glancing across the
table at his grandmother.

"You heard me. Why have you been sitting here for the
past . . ." she glanced up at the clock on her mantel, "hour,
purposely losing at piquet?"

Her grandson raised an eyebrow. "I admit that my play has been deplorable, but I assure you that I'm not—"

"Point. I win. Out with it, boy."

The problem with Grandmama Elizabeth, James reflected as he sighed and dropped his cards on the table, was that she always knew when something was going on. "I need a small favor."

"It being?"

"I'd like you to ask the Grahams to your box at the opera on Thursday night."

His grandmother narrowed her light green eyes. "And what will you be doing on Thursday night? A little larceny?"

"Please. I'm respectable now, remember? I'll be at the opera with you and the Grahams, of course."

She looked at him for a moment. "Why?"

James shrugged and gathered the cards together to shuffle them. "Does there have to be a reason? They're practically part of the family, after all." He glanced up to find she was frowning at him. "Won't do, hm?"

Grandmama Elizabeth shook her head. "For Simon, perhaps. Not you."

"All right, but don't bite my head off. It wasn't my idea."

"I'm listening."

"Simon asked if I'd pretend to fall in love with Angelique so that her parents would become nervous and agree to move up the wedding date." James sat back and crossed his arms.

The dowager viscountess blinked. "He what?" The marquis started to answer, but she waved a hand at him, apparently not expecting a response. "Simon asked you, and you agreed to this?"

"Well, against my better judgment. He rather convinced me that I owed him a favor."

"But Angelique?"

James gave a short grin, enjoying seeing Elizabeth Talbott nonplussed for a change. "Oh, she knows all about it."

"She does," his grandmother repeated faintly.

"Yes. But the Season's nearly over, and they haven't much time left. So An—Lady Angelique—informed her parents that I'd invited them to the opera on Thursday. So will you second the invitation for me?''

"And what of Simon?"

"I'm certain Lady Angelique has informed him all about it. But the Grahams will have to accept the invitation only if it comes from you.''

"And then what?"

James shrugged. "They are the schemers. I exist only to do their bidding." He grimaced. "The one independent thing I attempted was to invite Niston to have his family holiday with us at Abbonley, and he turned me down flat.''

Grandmama Elizabeth raised an eyebrow. "You invited guests to Abbonley?'' She looked truly surprised, and considering that since parting from Desiree he had never once even invited his nearest neighbors for tea, he could understand her amazement.

"The boy, Henry, wanted to see the stables," he offered, though it seemed a poor reason. "And I thought Simon and Lady Angelique would appreciate my efforts." He couldn't admit that for a fleeting moment he'd simply wanted the company. Her company. James shrugged. "Not that it amounted to much.''

"Thursday night, eh?" Grandmama Elizabeth queried after a moment. "*Don Giovanni*." She sighed. "At least I'll have your nonsense to keep me entertained.''

James grinned. "Thank you, Grandmama.''

She picked up the cards and began dealing. "Oh, I wouldn't miss this.''

On Thursday evening Abbonley even thought to send his own coach to pick them up. It had been ages since Angel had attended the opera, and she changed her gown four times before she found one that pleased her. Belatedly she remembered that she hadn't actually said anything about the evening to Simon, and she hoped Abbonley would make certain he appeared. This was for the two of them, after all, for their wedding.

When they arrived, the viscountess and Lord Abbonley

were already there. Angelique gave a smile as the marquis rose to take her hand. He was dressed in black and gray, and looked magnificent. "Lady Angelique," he said softly, and brought her fingers up to his lips. "I'm pleased you could attend tonight."

She curtsied, then after a moment remembered to retrieve her hand. "Good evening," she returned, taking a breath.

They had barely seated themselves when she noticed that the patrons in the audience below had begun murmuring, and dozens of pairs of opera glasses turned in their direction. She leaned toward Abbonley. "Where is Simon?" she whispered.

"I don't know," he returned, glancing down at his libretto. "Didn't you tell him about tonight?"

"Me?" she retorted quietly. "You're his cousin. Why didn't you—"

"This was your idea, my lady." The marquis raised his head and looked over at her speculatively. "You and Simon don't seem to communicate very well."

"We communicate splendidly," she shot back, angry that he appeared to be correct.

"What, dear?" her mother queried, turning to look at the two of them and stifling an obvious frown.

"Lady Angelique and I were discussing whether the number of waltzes at Almack's should be limited or not," James stepped in smoothly.

"You were?" Lady Elizabeth queried, raising an eyebrow.

"Just curious," the marquis affirmed. "Trying to catch up on London trends, you know."

"We were both in agreement that the patronesses are at least twenty years behind the times," Angelique, grateful for the assistance, added with a smile.

James grinned back. "The dance scarcely causes a raised eyebrow anymore in Paris."

"Exactly," Angel agreed, "and I don't see why—"

"We are not in Paris," Angel's mother put in shortly.

The marquis looked at her. "No, Lady Niston, we are not." He smiled again, looking over at Angelique. "And it is a resounding shame. Your daughter would be the belle of the city.''

His emerald eyes danced as he spoke, and Angel was glad to know this was only a charade. It was difficult to accept that someone who didn't believe in love could be so proficient at utilizing its trappings.

''My daughter is engaged,'' Angel's mother said succinctly.

The marquis sat back. ''An almost-married woman is not supposed to be thought of as attractive?'' he queried, his eyes still on Angelique.

The curtain rose before her mother could muster a response to that, and Angel rather thought that she might have liked the opera if she hadn't been so distracted with looking over at the marquis, to see whether he was enjoying himself.

At intermission Lady Elizabeth ordered Abbonley to go fetch her a glass of claret, and he reluctantly rose to comply. The viscountess looked over at Angelique, the light green eyes holding hers for a long moment. The old woman gave a slight nod, as if to herself. ''You know,'' she said, shifting her gaze to Angel's parents, ''Simon and I've been discussing having a house party at Abbonley to welcome James home. I'd like you to join us. We are to be family next year, after all.''

Niston cleared his throat. ''I don't—''

''Thomas,'' Lady Elizabeth interrupted, ''James mentioned that your son is interested in horses. You know Abbonley has one of the finest stables in England.'' Her expression softened a little. ''And whether the engagement is public knowledge or not, it is a fact, and I think our young couple deserves a celebration.'' She glanced at Angel's mother. ''Don't you?''

Her parents looked at one another, plainly displeased. ''We would be honored, Elizabeth,'' Camellia said, giving a stiff smile.

The marquis returned a moment later and handed over his grandmother's wine. ''This is why some people have servants, you know,'' he muttered, taking his seat again.

"Jamie, I've asked the Grahams to come visit us at Abbonley after the Season," Elizabeth informed him. "I thought we might have a party for Angelique and Simon."

James looked at her for a moment, something unreadable crossing his features. "Well, I'm pleased to hear it," he said, turning to Niston with a smile.

"Hm. Very good," the earl muttered as the lights dimmed and the curtain rose again.

"James, come with me to White's," Simon cajoled, stepping into the library.

James looked up from the book he was reading, where it seemed he'd been on the same page for a rather lengthy period of time. "I told you," he said, "I'm occupied." He stretched his bad leg, making a show of wincing even though it didn't bother him all that much anymore.

Simon was apparently unmoved. "So now you're a hermit, are you?"

"I believe I shall become one, yes," he returned with a slight grin.

"Except for the opera the other night."

"That was your darling betrothed's idea. Don't blame me."

"It still would have been nice if one of you had thought to inform me."

"Well, then, did someone inform you that the Grahams will be holidaying with us at Abbonley?" James commented, wishing to forestall any further miscommunications.

Simon raised an eyebrow. "What? How in the world did you arrange that?"

"It was Grandmama's idea," James explained, deciding it better if he didn't mention that he'd made the same offer, himself.

His cousin dropped into the other chair before the fire. "But that's splendid. I can continue to see Angel, and we can continue pressing her parents."

"It all does fall into place rather well," James commented, wondering for an odd, elated moment if Angelique would look upon Abbonley with the same delight as he.

Simon grinned. "Absolutely."

The affair at the Tremaines was to be the last grand ball of the Season. Upon her arrival Angel was cornered by Louisa and Mary, who proceeded to question her about her invitation to Abbonley. "Lady Elizabeth thought it would be pleasant to have some of the marquis's friends welcome him home," she replied.

"But no one goes to Abbonley," Mary protested.

Louisa nodded agreement and glanced dramatically about the room. "They say the marquis even ordered Simon not to go inside while he was overseeing it," she muttered.

"Well, that's rather silly, don't you think?" Angel pointed out.

Louisa opened her mouth to respond, then abruptly snapped it shut again.

A hand slid around Angel's elbow. "Lady Angelique," Abbonley greeted her with a sly smile, "my grandmother's been looking for you."

Abruptly realizing what had curbed Louisa's tongue, Angel nodded up at him. "Excuse me," she said to the two girls, relieved at the interruption. "Afraid I'll begin more rumors?" she muttered out of one side of her mouth as she stepped away with him.

He grinned. "One can never be too careful. Actually, though, I had a question for you."

This should be interesting. "Yes?" she returned, smiling up at him.

He cleared his throat. "It's been over a week since you last introduced me to a potential spouse. I was wondering if you'd given up."

"But Hester Peachley fulfilled all of the requirements you gave me. Apparently she is perfect for you." Abbonley tilted his head at her, looking devilishly handsome, and Angelique wondered who in the world might be the perfect woman for such a rogue and why she hadn't for a moment wanted him to find her.

"You mean I need to add another specification to my list," he murmured.

Angel shrugged and pursed her lips. "It's *your* list."

The marquis chuckled. "I think a sense of humor would be agreeable," he admitted.

"Hm," Angel replied, glancing about the room. "Let me review this. You want someone demure," and she ticked the points off on her fingers, "from a good family, intelligent and with a sense of humor." She looked up at him. "Have I left anything out?"

"No, I believe that will do it."

The room was quite crowded, and Angel spent a long moment searching while the marquis waited patiently beside her. She could feel his interest and curiosity in the way he was studying her features, and she was determined to find the exact woman who would be both perfect and absolutely wrong for him. Finally Angel spied her, seated with her mother halfway across the room. "I've got one," she said triumphantly, and started over.

Unexpectedly Abbonley took her arm. "Just a moment."

"What is it?" she queried, surprised.

"You're not heading for Flora Dalmia, are you?"

Angel wrinkled her nose at him, disappointed that he'd guessed. "How did you know?"

He looked at her for a moment, a hint of humorous exasperation touching his lean features. "Just a hunch."

"Well, let go, and I'll introduce you," she urged.

He freed her elbow, but made no move to continue. "Absolutely not," he stated, shaking his head.

"But why not?"

"Miss Graham, I don't mean to be cruel, but Miss Dalmia is shaped rather like a teapot."

Despite her determination to remain solemn a laugh burst through Angel's lips, and she raised her fan to her face. "So a good figure is yet another requirement? You're becoming rather particular, my lord."

Abbonley looked down at her. "And I begin to think that you have been dishonest with me."

"Dishonest?" she returned, raising an eyebrow. "Are you calling me a liar?"

"I'm saying you never had any intention of helping me find a wife."

"Perhaps that is because I doubt your sincerity in looking for one."

He folded his arms. "How could you know that, when you've done nothing but point me at a flock of farmyard hens?"

Angel raised her chin. "Generally, sir, when one is looking for a wife, one does not make a list first. One meets a woman, becomes acquainted with her, and then decides whether he thinks they might be compatible."

The marquis didn't look impressed with her argument. "This, I take it, is a description of your and Simon's courtship?"

"Perhaps."

"It sounds dull."

Now she was offended. Their courtship might not have been extraordinary, and perhaps Simon hadn't swept her off her feet, but they suited quite well. "Why, because Simon didn't have a string of available females brought around so he could examine their teeth?" she snapped.

James laughed at her, and Angel lost her temper. "What I think, my lord, is that you're afraid."

His emerald eyes narrowed. "Afraid?" he murmured. "Of what, pray tell, my lady?"

"I think you loved Desiree Kensington, and she didn't love you, and you're afraid to make another mistake."

Slowly Abbonley dropped his arms, and his face turned quite pale. "Just to show you how much I care for your opinion," he returned in a very quiet, controlled voice, "I will marry the first single woman who comes through that door." He pointed at the side entrance to the ballroom.

Angelique was shocked. "What if she doesn't wish to marry you?"

"Oh, she will." He looked toward the doorway. "I can be quite charming. You said so, yourself."

"I won't have anything to do with this," she returned,

finally realizing that quite a few guests were looking their way, and that even if they had been pretending a seduction, she'd spent far too long speaking to him. She started to walk away, but he reached out to take her hand.

He brought her fingers to his lips in what looked like a polite gesture, but in truth he was holding her so tightly she would have had to wrestle him to break free. "Just a moment, my lady. We're not through with this game, yet."

Reluctantly Angel looked away from his grim expression toward the doorway. Mrs. Beadle entered on her husband's arm, and then the Countess of Devenbroke. "This is absurd," she whispered, trying to tug free. "Let me go and forget this. I apologize if I've made you angry."

The marquis kept his eyes on the entrance. A moment later he nodded and gave a slow, humorless smile. "There you are, Lady Angelique. It's done."

Angelique looked. "No!" she gasped as Lily Stanfred spied them from the doorway and came forward with a smile. "You can't be serious, my lord. She's not at all what you wanted."

"She is perfect, my lady. Demure, polite, intelligent, from a good family, and with a sense of humor or you'd never have her as a friend." Finally he looked down at her, his eyes cold. "Why didn't you send her my way before?"

"Because she . . . you . . ." Because Lily was exactly what the marquis had been looking for, she realized. "You are the Devil himself, sir," she said instead, fighting tears, "and I hate you."

She pulled away and intercepted her friend. "What's wrong, Angel?" Lily asked, putting a hand on her arm. "You're white as a sheet. Whatever were you and the marquis talking about?"

"Nothing," she returned, forcing a smile that felt ghastly. "I was just a little warm, and he was concerned."

Her friend eyed her closely. "You both looked rather angry to me," she offered, then smiled. "But that's none of my affair. Is your Simon in attendance tonight? He said there was a new country dance he wanted to teach me."

"Yes, he's here." Angel turned to look for him. Unfortunately the first sight that caught her eye was Abbonley in discussion with Lily's father, Lord Stanfred. The baron said something and nodded. The marquis glanced in her direction, then turned back with a smile and offered his hand to Lord Stanfred, who hurriedly took it.

"Oh, no," she whispered, wondering what in the world he was up to. He couldn't have meant his words seriously. It was completely absurd, even for someone who claimed not to believe in love.

"Angel."

At Simon's urgent tone, Angel jumped. "What is it?" she snapped.

For a moment Simon looked taken aback. "Have you seen James?" he muttered, glancing about.

"He's over there, with Lily's father," she returned. "I'm sorry if I snapped . . ." Angel trailed off, for it was obvious that Simon's attention was not on her. She turned to follow his gaze, then drew in a sharp breath.

Raven-haired Desiree Kensington stood just inside the curtained entryway. Her low-cut russet gown was by far the most daring ensemble in the room, and was being much admired both by her husband, the much older Lord Kensington, and by several other gentlemen of somewhat dubious reputation.

Abruptly Lady Kensington straightened, and at almost the same moment Abbonley turned and saw her. His complexion went white. The rising murmur of the other guests sounded like the hum of a beehive as they noticed the drama.

"Damnation," Simon breathed.

"James," Desiree exclaimed with a smile, attracting the attention of whomever had remained oblivious to the growing tension.

After a moment the marquis nodded, excused himself from Lord Stanfred, and strolled over to Desiree. Simon tensed, but James leaned down to take Lady Kensington's hand and raise it to his lips. She smiled and said something, but at his return smile and murmured response she paled and took a step away. He released her hand and, seeing Simon, walked over as the crowd parted to let him through.

"James," Simon whispered, "are you all right?"

"Fine," the marquis replied in a calm, unconcerned voice. A waltz began in the background, and as the marquis glanced about, Angelique saw loneliness and hurt in his eyes. She had been furious at him, but seeing his pain distressed her a great deal more than she had expected.

Lord Kensington appeared behind them, approaching at a gouty limp, face red and expression angry. If Angel had any say, there was not going to be a second duel over Desiree Kensington.

"James, this is our dance," she improvised quickly. Her promised dance partner would simply have to do without her.

James looked down at her, his expression blank. "Oh— of course," he replied, and led her onto the floor.

"I'm going to change your mind, you know," she ventured.

He started a little. "Beg pardon?"

"I said I'm going to change your mind. About Lily."

"Lady Angelique, I really don't wish to continue that argument at the moment," he said quietly, avoiding her eyes.

"All right," she acquiesced. "But you must realize that while she might fit your silly list, she's not at all what you need."

His expression darkened. "I doubt you have any idea what it is I need."

Angel thought the set-down completely uncalled for, especially after she had just rescued him from a scene. "I apologize, my lord, if I was wrong in thinking that you and I might possibly have become friends in the past few weeks. If my ideas and advice are not welcome to you, I shall not offer them again."

His gaze snapped down at her. After the briefest of moments he looked away again at Simon, watching them from the side of the ballroom, Lily beside him. "Friends," he repeated at a murmur. "Very well, my future cousin. I shall not be the first to back out of this arrangement. I don't have much honor left, but enough remains for me to be able to keep my word.''

The waltz ended and he returned her to her parents. Angel watched as he made his excuses to the Tremaines and then left the ball. Lady Kensington watched his departure as well, with cool, dark eyes. It might not be any of her concern, but Angel found that Desiree's interest in the Devil didn't please her at all.

James opted to ride Demon to Abbonley. Simon was mounted on Admiral, and the two of them set off ahead of a caravan of five coaches, one of which held Grandmama Elizabeth and a battery of smelling salts, and the others containing a great deal of her luggage.

Simon had kept nearly silent all morning, and James couldn't blame him. At least the evening had been a complete disaster, for he hated wasting his energy on partial ones. To say that he had been shocked at the sight of Desiree Langley—no, her name was Kensington, now—was an understatement. He hadn't realized she was in London, though in retrospect it had been foolish to assume her elsewhere. She was still a beauty, perhaps even more so than she had been. Five years ago when he had been in love with her, when he had killed a man over the issue of her heart, she had been a vision.

Whatever she had been to him, she was certainly not the reason he had hesitated to choose a wife, for he had decided to marry, after all. He was rather relieved, in fact, that the choice had been made. Despite Angelique's vehement protests, Miss Lily Stanfred did meet all of his requirements, and he was rather surprised that he hadn't noticed her earlier.

The whole thing might have been even worse than it turned out, for despite his anger he wasn't certain he could have gone through with his pronouncement if it had been Hester Peachley striding through that door. Besides, this way it would aggravate Angelique Graham no end, and sometimes that outspoken chit was completely beyond bearing. She had practically forced him into choosing Miss Stan-fred. And—

"James?"

He turned his head, wondering how long Simon had been speaking to him. "Sorry," he mumbled. "What is it?"

"What did you say to her?"

James frowned. "To whom?"

"To Desiree, of course."

"Simon . . ." he warned in a growl.

"All right," his cousin said, throwing up a hand. "Forget I asked. Never mind. Don't tell me."

"Sweet . . ." James muttered, glancing back at his grand-mother's carriage. "She said she was pleased to see me, and I told her to go to the devil." He paused, noting Simon's shocked expression, for it would never occur to his cousin to say such a thing to a woman. "I didn't think at the time that I was quite possibly referring to myself."

His cousin looked at him for a moment. "I hoped you thanked Angel for keeping you out of a scene," he said stiffly, "you trying to become respectable, and all."

"What do you mean?"

"The old baron, Kensington, was after you when you and Angel went out onto the floor. I hate to think what might have happened if he—" Simon blanched.

James looked at him, knowing exactly what his cousin was thinking. "I don't duel anymore, Simon. And certainly not over her." He looked away, taking a deep breath. "Did I tell you I've invited the Stanfreds to join us at Abbonley?"

Simon blinked. "When did this occur?"

"Last night. They'll be here in a fortnight or so." He grimaced, unexpectedly reluctant to speak of the true reason for their visit. His own state of matrimony was supposed to wait until after his cousin's had been settled, anyway. "I thought the Grahams might like the company. Keep them from feeling outnumbered and lull them into thinking this is an innocent outing."

Simon laughed, back in good humor again. "You make it

sound as though this is a military campaign.''

James raised an eyebrow. ''Isn't it?''

On the afternoon of their second day of travel they crossed the edge of his property, and he found himself looking about to make certain all of the trees, the streams, and the walls, hedges and tenant cottages were still there, still in place. Half an hour later they wound around a turn in the road and Abbonley came into view on top of the hill. At the sight of the great white horseshoe-shaped manor, he pulled Demon to an abrupt halt and sat staring up at it.

''Welcome back, James,'' Simon said softly from beside him.

James had to clear his throat twice before he could answer. ''By God, it's good to be home,'' he declared fervently, and Simon grinned.

7

"Is that it?" Henry asked, craning his head to look out the coach window. "Is that Abbonley?"

"I hope there's a pony for me to ride," Helen pouted, banging Millicent's head against the edge of the seat. "Angel got to bring Heaven."

"Buttercup couldn't have travelled this far," Camellia pointed out patiently.

"Papa, is that Abbonley?" Henry yelled, waving his arm outside the coach.

"We'll know in a moment," Lord Niston replied from his mount.

Angelique settled back in the cushions, taking deep breaths and trying to quell the fluttering of her stomach, which manifested every time Henry asked if that was Abbonley ahead. She told herself it was because she was looking forward to seeing Simon and working on their plan, but knew it had more to do with the marquis. She wasn't entirely certain whether they had parted friends or not, but she was not about to let him marry Lily Stanfred just to spite his future cousin.

"It is Abbonley, isn't it!" Henry yelled, leaning precariously out the window. "Oh, it's grand! Can you see the stables, Papa?"

Angel couldn't resist any longer, and she leaned forward to look around Henry's shoulders. A huge white manor sprawled atop a gently sloping hill. At the foot of the rise a lake opened across a clearing, hemmed at the shore by a sizeable glade. It was breathtaking.

In half an hour they were at the head of the drive. The huge oak double doors opened, and the marquis, followed by a retinue of footmen, strode out to greet them. "Welcome to Abbonley," he said, coming forward to shake her father's hand. "I trust you had a pleasant trip?"

"Quite so," Lord Niston replied.

That was fine for him to say, Angel thought, for he hadn't had to ride with the twins.

"And how was your journey?" Abbonley queried, strolling over to brush her knuckles with his lips.

"Noisy," she replied, smiling. "As usual."

"I see you brought Heaven," he noted, giving a smile of his own. "There is some fine riding here. I think you'll enjoy it, my lady."

"Thank you, my lord," she responded, studying his face. He seemed a little more relaxed than the last time she had seen him, and when Brutus bounded out of the coach to place his paws on the marquis' chest, Abbonley actually laughed.

"I was hoping you'd brought your monster along," he chuckled, ruffling the mastiff's ears. "Simon will be thrilled."

Angel hadn't thought Simon all that fond of her pet. "Where is Simon?"

"He'll be along in a moment," the marquis answered offhandedly, and then swept a bow to the twins. "Master Henry, Lady Helen, Millicent," he greeted them, and Angel was surprised he had remembered her siblings' names, much less that of Helen's doll. James Faring surprised her quite a bit, though, when he wasn't being completely aggravating.

"My lord marquis," Henry returned, bowing nearly double.

The Devil leaned down. "James will be fine," he muttered, grinning.

Henry gasped, and Angelique turned to follow his gaze toward the side of the manor. Simon came around the corner leading an undersized but perfectly proportioned chestnut gelding and a small black mare.

"Henry, Helen, meet India and Jasmine," James said.

Angel expected Henry to bolt for the pony, but he walked slowly up to the animal and talked to it for a moment before he raised his hand to pet it, much as James had done when he was introduced to Pharaoh. She looked sideways at James. "If I might ask, what is the Marquis of Abbonley doing with two children's mounts in his famous stables?"

He gave her an innocent look. "I couldn't very well promise and then disappoint, now could I?" He raised an eyebrow. "Should I have brought you a pony as well?"

"I am not as easy to win over as the twins, my lord," she responded, feeling she had scored a hit.

"And the greater the challenge, the greater the reward," he murmured, flashing his wicked grin at her, "my lady."

She blushed, which would have been entirely too silly except that her parents had to have noticed.

Simon approached, smiling. "You look radiant, Angel," he said, taking her hand. "How was your journey?"

"Thank you, Simon," she said warmly, shooting an annoyed look over his head at Abbonley, who had the bad manners to chuckle. "It was quite pleasant."

The marquis turned to her father again. "Shall we go inside?" he suggested. "As it's so warm today, I'm having luncheon set out in the courtyard, but I thought you might like to go to your rooms first." This last was directed at Angel's mother, who nodded gratefully.

Angelique was more than curious to see inside Abbonley. As they reached the door she felt an inkling of uneasiness, for the butler was quite possibly the sternest, most dour-looking personage she had ever set eyes on. What she saw inside, however, surprised her. It was dark and elegant, but the curtains were open and there were fresh flowers everywhere, making the rooms smell like springtime and giving the manor a cozy warmth. She couldn't help smiling.

Simon escorted her to one of the rooms in the west wing, while the marquis showed her parents and siblings to neighboring bed chambers. "James and I are in the east wing," Simon explained, motioning along the curving balcony behind them, "but Grandmama is two doors down from you, for she doesn't like the morning sun. When Lily arrives she'll be next to you, here."

"Lily?" Angel queried, trying to hide her sudden surprised dismay.

"Oh, yes. James didn't tell you? He's invited the Stanfreds along, as well. Thought you might enjoy the company."

Angelique forced a smile. "That was kind of him."

Simon smiled as well. "Yes, I thought so. He's being rather more cooperative than I'd expected." He kissed her knuckles again. "Someone shall be by to bring you down to the courtyard."

She stepped into the room, and wasn't surprised to see more flowers sitting on the stand by the bed. The chamber was decorated in gold and peach, and she liked it immediately. Fleetingly, she wondered if James had chosen which room she would occupy. From the window she had a splendid view of the south end of the lake and of the woods beyond, and until Tess came in to help her freshen up she sat in the sill and looked out at the water, a blue reflection of the sky.

Outside in the courtyard a long table had been set with fresh fruit, sliced ham and chicken, and several desserts that immediately had her mouth watering. She wasn't the only one impressed with the confections, either, for when Henry and Helen appeared a moment later they bolted for that end of the table.

"Luncheon first, you two," she said, wishing she could head straight for the strawberry creams resting tantalizingly on a silver platter.

The marquis was already present, listening to a report given by the head footman. After a moment he nodded and strolled over to her. "Are you pleased with your accommodations?"

She nodded. "Quite," she answered, wondering why the

more at ease he seemed, the more unsettled she became. London might have been her territory, but Abbonley was definitely his.

"Lord James?" Henry said hesitantly, and the marquis turned.

"Master Henry?"

"Do you boat on the lake?"

The marquis looked thoughtful for a moment. "You know, we used to have several rowboats," he answered slowly, "but this end of the lake's become a bit swampy, and I can't for the life of me remember what's happened to them. I'll check with Simon, and see if there isn't something we can't do. I haven't been fishing in quite awhile."

"There are fish?" Henry asked, his eyes lighting.

"Oh, yes. When I was younger I caught supper on a regular basis."

"Henry, Helen, come sit down and eat," Camellia called from one of the tables that had been set up in the shade of the west wing.

"You shouldn't have told him that," Angel commented as the marquis took a plate from one of the servants and handed it to her before he accepted another for himself.

"Why not?" he asked, indicating that she should select her luncheon.

"He'll nag you incessantly, now," she told him, picking up a strawberry cream and then a second. Strawberries and horses were her greatest weaknesses.

"Take another," he suggested, seeming to read her mind, and reached over to place a third one on her plate.

Immediately Angel was distrustful of his solicitude. "Are you trying to cushion the blow before you inform me that you've invited the Stanfreds here?"

He raised an eyebrow. "Lady Angelique, I really don't need to inform you of anything. This is *my* estate, and I may invite whomever I choose to come and visit me." Angel scowled, and he raised a hand. "I don't wish to argue with you."

"Well, why not?" she demanded, primed for a fight.

James gave a short grin. "Because, much as I enjoy sallying with you, I do prefer seeing you smile," he said softly.

That stopped her. "Oh," she managed.

"And I was being nice because I wanted to thank you," he went on.

She looked up at him. "For what?"

"I was rather . . . distracted at the Tremaines. You were very kind, and I apologize for snapping at you." For a brief moment his expression darkened. "What is between Desiree and me is not for public view, whatever she might think."

She was tempted to ask what exactly was between Lady Kensington and him. Instead she frowned and squinted, trying to look ignorant. Acknowledging her part would be decidedly unladylike, and the more proper she was, the less excuse her parents would have to delay the wedding. "I accept your thanks," she began, "though I'm not quite certain why, as it was you claimed my hand for the waltz."

He looked down at her, and after a moment pursed his lips and nodded. "Ah. How forgetful of me. Thank you again, my future cousin," he remarked, then excused himself to take a seat.

Angel had only a moment to wonder why she was coming to dislike that particular epithet before Simon reached her side. "How do you like Abbonley?" he asked as he accepted a plate.

"It's magnificent," she said with a smile.

"Yes," he agreed ruefully. "I'm afraid it will make the estate at Turbin Hall look quite shabby. Perhaps I should never have shown you James's treasure."

Angel touched his sleeve, wishing people would stop referring to her future home as mouldy and shabby. "You've done a grand job here, Simon."

Simon grimaced. "James has done a grand job. I can take credit only for maintaining it while he was away."

"Well, you've done that grandly," she insisted stubbornly, and he smiled at her.

"You are too kind, Angel."

"Sounds like a reasonable enough compliment to me,"

the viscountess said from behind her. Lady Elizabeth piled strawberries on a plate held by one of the footmen. "I'm pleased you've come, child."

"Thank you for inviting us, Lady Elizabeth," Angel responded with a smile.

"Nonsense," the dowager viscountess snapped, eyes twinkling. "Jamie, come here and greet your grandmother," she demanded.

The marquis obediently rose and strolled over to kiss Lady Elizabeth on the cheek. "Bossy," he murmured.

"Scamp," the viscountess replied in the same tone.

Elizabeth took a seat with Angel and Simon at the second table, and the luncheon conversation was lively, to say the least. By the end of the meal Angel's sides hurt from laughing. Simon for the most part stayed out of the good-natured bantering between the marquis and his grandmother, but Angel had already noted that bantering didn't seem to be Simon's style. It was James Faring's, however, and unfortunately, and to the annoyance of her parents, hers.

James offered a tour of the stables, much to the delight of both Henry and Angelique. After inviting the boy to go riding in the morning he regretfully excused himself to go inside and find Algers, his agent, waiting for him in the study. Simon had done a fine job with Abbonley, but there were still details that needed to be taken care of, things that had been delayed until his return and that he now wanted done. The school in the village of Esterley, which sat on the edge of his land, had been erected in his absence, but awaited his approval before it could be occupied. It was a special project of his, and he determined to visit it before the end of the week.

Finally Algers, burdened with enough tasks to keep him busy for a fortnight, departed. James sat back with a sigh. It used to be that he detested taking care of the details of the estate, especially in the year right after his father's death when he had returned from London to find Abbonley in disarray, and the countryside mourning the death of Richard

Faring and dreading having his wild son ensconced in his place.

Now it was a task he rather enjoyed, seeing the progression of things he had planned. The school was a prime example. His neighboring landowners might think him a fool for educating the laborers on his property, but he hadn't seen any evidence that keeping them ignorant did any good.

Simon knocked and leaned into the room. "Is Algers gone?"

James chuckled. "I told you, you don't have to deal with him any longer."

His cousin came into the room and seated himself. "It's only that he's so opinionated. Made me feel every decision I made was going to send Abbonley sliding into the lake."

James pushed against the window sill. "We still seem to be anchored fairly firmly," he said with a grin. "Which reminds me. What happened to the rowboats I used to have?"

"Heavens, I don't know. They've probably been beached somewhere along the lake." Simon sat back and crossed his ankles. "You surprised me when you gave in to Grandmama, you know. I'm pleased you've finally decided to allow guests into Abbonley."

James gazed out the window. "Being alone isn't quite as attractive as it used to be." He took a seat, mulling over whether or not he should bring up a subject that had been nagging at him for several weeks. "Why didn't you ever tell me that my . . . antics were damaging your reputation, as well?"

Frowning, Simon rose halfway to his feet. "Now look, James—"

James gestured at him. "I'm not implying anything. I was just curious. Because you can't tell me that my being your relation didn't have something to do with the Grahams putting off this wedding for as long as they could possibly manage."

Simon slowly took his seat again. "I don't know, James. I suppose I didn't think you would listen."

The marquis looked at his cousin for a long moment. "I

probably wouldn't have." He stood again, pacing back to the window. "But what if I don't want to be the Devil any longer, Simon? What if I want to change?"

"Change?" Simon repeated skeptically. "You've been not changing for five years. More than that if you count your, and my, misspent youth."

"Well, I'm trying now," James returned. "I haven't had a drink in six months, and I've been doing my damndest to behave."

"I didn't know that," Simon said after a moment.

"Didn't know what?"

"That you'd stopped drinking. Now that you mention it, I should have. Your temperament has been more even since you returned from fighting Bonaparte. I wasn't expecting . . ." he trailed off, looking embarrassed.

James shrugged. "You had no reason to notice. But I recently had a great deal of time to do some thinking, and decided I didn't particularly like where I was heading."

"In the army hospital?"

He shook his head. "Before that, mainly." He cleared his throat. "When . . . when I was wounded at Waterloo, I slid down into a damned muddy ditch. One of my sergeants landed across me with a lance through him. It was chaos there for awhile, and anyway . . . I was left for dead."

"My God," Simon whispered.

"I lay there for two days before one of the grave-diggers found me." He turned to see Simon staring at him, white-faced. "I had a great deal of time to do nothing but consider my situation." He looked away. "The whole episode was quite enlightening, actually."

"I hope so," his cousin returned slowly.

James forced a smile. "That doesn't mean I've become some sort of bloody saint," he muttered.

"That would be too much to expect," Simon agreed, smiling when James glared at him.

"Very amusing." James looked out the window once more, then at the sight of the Graham ladies touring his garden, turned and headed for the door. "I would appreciate, however, if from this point you would make an effort to acknowledge my no-doubt amateurish and half-hearted attempts at respectability.''

"I shall do my best, cousin," Simon answered dutifully.

Supper passed relatively uneventfully, though James was coming to realize that few things seemed to be uneventful where the Grahams, and especially their eldest daughter, were concerned. His eyes kept going to her, for she looked especially lovely in a dark peach gown that brought out the red highlights in her hair. Whenever he realized he was staring he deliberately turned away, but that did nothing to keep the girl out of his mind. In fact, he'd been having impure thoughts about her since he'd first set eyes on her in Dover. James glanced over at his cousin. The only thing he could do about that was to make certain Simon never even suspected.

The next morning before breakfast he went down to the stables and found Henry, and surprisingly, Angelique, there waiting for him. He had the horses and pony saddled, and the three of them, and Brutus, started off toward the lake. India was a well-bred animal, and had cost him a prize mare in trade, but the delighted look on the boy's face as he rode along made it worth the price. When the two had settled, he nudged the restless Demon into a trot. The gray mare, Heaven, easily kept pace beside them, and he noted that Angel was holding her back. "Ready for a bit more, Henry?"

The woods at the edge of the lake were still covered with the morning's dew, and mist hung in the tops of the trees. It was his favorite time of day, and he had dreamt of riding the trail while he had recuperated in France. In those visions he had been alone, however, not accompanied by a nine-year-old boy, his madcap sister and a large brown mastiff. Feeling almost domestic, he looked at Angelique.

"Enjoying the view?" he asked.

She smiled at him. "It's beautiful here."

"Yes, it is," he replied, looking straight at her. He wasn't surprised when instead of blushing she shook her head and laughed at him. It seemed that if he had seriously intended to seduce her, a fresh approach would have been required. Old methods, which had netted high flyers far less naive than she, merely seemed to amuse Angel. Of course she would never take his advances seriously anyway, for they both knew his purpose was only to get her married to Simon as soon as they could manage it.

He guided them north toward the main road and finally up the winding, tree-lined drive to Abbonley. It was a shorter ride than he liked, but he didn't want to tire Henry or India on their first outing together. "Do you enjoy his paces?" he asked the boy when they had reached the path to the stables.

"He's top of the trees, Lord James. Does he jump?"

James laughed, wondering where the boy had learned that expression. His sister, most likely. "We'll give it a try tomorrow."

"Yes, please!"

Niston was waiting for them when they returned, and Henry was clearly bursting to tell him all about their excursion. James turned to see Angel eyeing the stables reluctantly. "What is it?" he asked, though he could guess.

"Oh, nothing," she answered, sighing.

"I have to ride down to the village and inspect the new school, he said, pulling Demon in a tight circle when the horse threatened to continue their morning's ride without him. "I thought to do it this morning. Do you wish to accompany me?" he asked, though he hadn't until that moment decided to go.

The reluctant look cleared from her face. "If you don't mind. I've done nothing but sit in a coach for two days," she noted with her usual candor.

"Angel, I think your mother—" Niston began with a frown, glancing from James to his daughter.

James understood the look. "Hastings?" he yelled for the head groom. "Saddle up! We're riding into Esterley."

Thomas cleared his throat. "Very good," he muttered, turning to follow his son when Henry insisted on helping put up India.

"Splendidly done," Angel whispered, grinning at him.

It was a moment before he realized what she was talking about. He inclined his head. "Of course, my lady. Anything for the cause."

Once Hastings appeared, James led the way east. With a glance at Angel, he kicked Demon into a run. In a moment she and Heaven were thundering behind them, and he noted again that she was a fine rider. The mare was no match for Demon, however, and after a mile or so he slowed and allowed her to catch up.

Angelique was laughing, her bonnet blown back off her head and her copper hair flying around her face. She was breathtaking. "Better?" he asked, all his pure and brotherly thoughts toward her crumbling into dust. This holiday was going to be even more difficult than seeing her in London, he abruptly realized. And with them in the same house, there was nowhere for him to run.

Angel nodded vigorously, obviously unconscious as to the knots she was making of his insides. "Much. How far is the village?"

"About another two miles, beyond the rise there," he answered, pointing. She nodded, then with a laugh sent Heaven into a gallop. He gave her a head start, then, grinning, turned Demon after them.

The wood and brick school had been erected on the east edge of the village. As they made their way through Esterley, James was greeted by the dozen or so villagers out and about in the cold morning. He returned the welcomes with a smile, for he hadn't had much time to come into the village since his return to Abbonley.

"You are well-liked here," Angelique stated as he swung out of the saddle and stepped around to help her down from Heaven. Behind them Brutus bounded up the steps into the school, then appeared at one of the windows to bark at them.

"Surprised?" he queried, letting his hands linger around her waist for a moment.

She tried to straighten her hat again and looked up at him. "No." Hastings rode up behind them, and she turned to face the school. "So tell me about your project, my lord," she commented, stepping up to peer into a window.

He handed Demon's reins over to the groom and followed her around the front of the building. "I merely thought it made sense to educate my tenants."

"It doesn't to a great many other landowners, I'll wager," Angelique noted, folding her hands behind her back and critically eyeing the brickwork.

He glanced over at her. Angelique Graham might be something of a madcap, but she was certainly far from one of those empty-headed trinkets who simpered their way through their debuts every Season. "And what do you think?"

"I think the London wags failed to note several significant things about you," she commented, pausing to watch him as he stepped back to eye the structure from a distance.

"It's not one of the more exciting things I've done, I'm afraid," he agreed.

"One of the best, though, ye ask me, milord," Hastings put in stoutly.

The construction looked solid from the outside, and he knew Hastings had gone several times to view the building. His youngest son would be one of the children attending the school. "Thank you," James replied, smiling.

Brutus reappeared and reared up on Angelique's shoulders, favoring her with a sloppy kiss on one cheek. "Brutus!" she admonished, stumbling backward, and James quickly stepped forward to catch her before she could fall.

Her silky copper hair spilled out over his arm as her hat came loose, and she looked up at him with a grin. "My hero," she chuckled. "I keep telling Brutus to be certain to have all four legs on the ground at all times, but I don't think he understands."

He found himself lost in her sparkling hazel eyes. To cover his abrupt discomfiture, James quickly scooped her back upright and then bent to retrieve her hat. When he glanced at Angelique she was dabbing at her damp cheek with an embroidered handkerchief.

"How's that?" she inquired.

"Perfect," he returned. Stepping forward, he took the handkerchief from her. "That's the one you were working on in the coach, isn't it?" he queried. "I don't think the roses turned out crooked at all."

She looked up at him curiously. "You remembered that?"

"I remember everything about you." Her eyes remained on him as he held her gaze. After a moment she turned away again, almost quickly enough to hide her blush. As she disappeared up the steps into the school, he wondered if Angelique realized that sometime this morning, flirting with her had ceased to be a game.

8

Simon paced in front of the stables as they approached. "You rode early," he said, frowning as he came forward to help Angel dismount. He was dressed to ride, she noted with dismay.

"I wanted to show Lady Angelique my school," the marquis returned before she could answer, stepping around her and heading for the manor. "She's quite progressive-minded," he continued over his shoulder.

He seemed in a hurry to leave them. Angel gazed after him, not certain whether to be vexed or amused. She turned back to see Simon wiping a disapproving look off his face, and she tried again to straighten her hat. "It's a nice school," she declared. It had impressed her, as had the marquis's obvious interest and pride in the structure, and the good he thought it would do for the local children.

"Another of James's foolish and impetuous ideas," Simon said, obviously out of countenance with the two of them.

"Simon, you should have seen Papa's face when your cousin asked me to go riding," she soothed. "If this continues, we could be married by Christmas."

Simon gave a reluctant smile. "Sooner than that, hopefully." He gripped her fingers. "But tomorrow you must ride with me."

She smiled back. "Of course."

For the next few days, in fact, she rode with Simon, he choosing mid-morning as more suitable to her delicate sensibilities. It gave her little chance to ride as she would have liked, as she had ridden with James, but she said nothing. That hadn't been at all proper, and she would simply have to get used to the idea of doing without galloping.

The morning before the Stanfreds were to arrive she rose later than usual, and had to rush to dress in her blue riding habit and meet Simon. "Master Simon," Hastings greeted them as he came out of the stables. "My lady."

"Good morning, Hastings. Saddle Admiral and Heaven, if you please."

As the groom nodded and turned for the stables, James emerged mounted on the hunter, Pharaoh. With a nod at them and a kick, he sent the stallion off at a gallop toward the lake.

"He's a grand rider, ain't he?" Henry's admiring voice came from the manor path, echoing her own thoughts. She'd been curious to try Pharaoh herself, though she hadn't found an opportunity to bring it up with the marquis.

"Henry, why don't you stay here with Hastings?" Simon unexpectedly suggested. "He'll help you practice your jumps."

In the blink of an eye Henry's stubborn and disappointed look turned to a pleased smile. "Would you, Hastings?"

The grizzled head groom grinned at him. "My pleasure, Master Henry."

As soon as they were mounted, Simon started them off at a sedate trot along the lake path. "Are you enjoying Abbonley?"

Angel nodded. "It's enchanting," she smiled, gazing over to her right where she could just see the glitter of the lake through the trees.

"My father's estate at Wansglen is a great deal like this, though not nearly so grand." He glanced over at her. "Of course Turbin Hall is quite interesting, as well. Have I told you it still has some of the original furniture from when Henry the Eighth came to visit my great-grandfather?"

"It . . . hasn't been touched at all since then, you mean?" Angel queried.

"Oh, heavens no. Grandmama refers to it as the Talbott museum." He gave a short smile. "None of this modernizing James is so fascinated with. Windows, for example. With the tax on them, how many does one actually need? And yet James even had more put in for his kitchens. I'll admit that some innovations might be handy, but after awhile a place loses its sense of history, don't you think?"

"Oh, of course," Angel returned weakly. She'd several times complained that her mother treated Niston like a museum, where no one was supposed to move a stick of furniture without first conferring with all the ancestral bones buried in the family cemetery. And Niston was less than half as old as Turbin Hall.

When they reached the picturesque stone bridge that spanned the stream by the far side of the lake, Simon unexpectedly stopped and dismounted, then stepped over to help her down as well. He took Angel's hand and led her over to sit on the low wall of the bridge beside him.

"I'm pleased you came here," he said, "and I hope that this plan with James hasn't offended you. I know he can be something of a . . . rakehell, I suppose is the word."

"Not at all," she answered truthfully, for she enjoyed the marquis's spirited company, and his flirting. He wasn't at all high in the instep like many of the titled English. Apparently, being a rake had its advantages. Sometimes she wished she could emulate him, for then she could behave as she fancied, and hang the consequences.

"That pleases me," Simon commented, obviously not reading her thoughts. With that, he took her chin in his hand and drew her face toward his, then kissed her gently on the lips. He repeated the action, then sat back a little. "It's been far too long since we did that last," he said.

"When you proposed to me?" she returned, smiling. Jenny Smith had told her last Season that being kissed was like thunder and lightning, but Jenny could be rather silly and believed all of those giddy novels she read. Kissing

Simon reminded her of a gentle breeze, calm and safe and steady. And, she admitted for the first time, rather less than exciting.

That thought unexpectedly left her quite sad, and she took her leave of Simon once they returned to the manor, only to find that her family had driven into Esterley with Lady Elizabeth. She walked through the garden, trying to lighten her lowered spirits, but nothing helped. If their plan was working as well as they believed, they could be married by the end of the year. She should be ecstatic. Instead, she felt unaccountably lonely. She left the garden and went inside, wandering through the multitude of elegant rooms.

Finally she found herself outside her favorite room at Abbonley. The library door was open so she walked in, heading straight for the closest of the tall, narrow windows that looked out over the garden. For several minutes she sat there, gazing out pensively.

"What troubles you, Angelique?"

Angel nearly jumped out of her skin. She whipped her head around to see the marquis seated in one of the overstuffed chairs close to the fireplace, his gleaming Hessian boots stretched out in front of him with ankles crossed and a book in one hand.

Blushing furiously at being caught moping like a peagoose, she started to rise. "I'm sorry," she stammered, "I didn't know you were in here."

He waved her back toward the sill. "Don't leave on my account. Just taking advantage of the lull." James looked at her closely for a moment, making her wonder again if he could read her thoughts. "Would you like a glass of Madeira or something?"

"It's a bit early for that, don't you think?" she returned testily.

He glanced up at the clock on the mantel, then shrugged in his single-shouldered way. "I suppose so." He smiled a little grimly. "I was never much good at remembering what hours were socially acceptable for drinking."

"And now?" she asked, intrigued by his comment.

"And now I don't have to worry about it," he replied. "Part of my reformation, you know."

"That's good, I think," she commented quietly.

"Thank you," he answered, then cocked his head at her, his eyes studying her face. "You haven't answered my question."

"Which question?"

"What troubles you?" he repeated softly.

Angelique looked back out the window and shrugged. "I don't know. I just thought something would be a certain way, and it wasn't."

He nodded. "I've found that to be true of a great many things," he responded, typically cynical.

She lifted her chin. "You mean Desiree?" she asked boldly.

Several emotions, not all of them pleasant, played across his lean features. "Do I have a lantern above my head that lights every time you say that name, or something?" he finally asked.

"That's a bit absurd, don't you think?" she responded, relieved that he wasn't shouting.

"I am simply trying to figure out why you relate every minuscule particle of my conversation to my sordid past with Desiree Kensington. You use her name like a knife blade, you know."

"I do no such thing."

"You do," he argued. "And I'd rather you fling the spear of Miss Peachley in my direction, if you don't mind."

That only served to remind her that he'd selected Lily Stanfred as his future bride. "I'd fling neither at you if only you'd let Lily alone," she returned.

James Faring sat back and looked at her. "Am I so horrible that you can't stand even the thought of your friend being wed to me?" he queried. "Would I be such a terrible husband?"

"Yes," she answered, rising and moving to the fireplace. There was a lovely pair of Egyptian–style candlesticks there, and she lifted one to examine it.

"Why?"

"Because she's all wrong for you. Lily is very . . . nice. And you would be completely bored with her. Unless you like to speak of the latest Paris fashions or the weather."

She felt James walk over to stand behind her. "That's not a very kind description of a friend," he murmured in his dry voice. "Besides, I asked why I was wrong for her, not why she was wrong for me."

Angelique found that she didn't want to move. Her fingers stilled on the polished brass of the candlestick, her eyes half closed as she listened to the sound of his voice. "Did you?"

"I did," he continued. "You almost sound as though you're more concerned with my happiness than with Miss Stanfred's."

"I . . ." Angelique shook herself. "I don't need to be concerned with your happiness, because you don't believe in love."

She turned to look up at him. For a moment she stood frozen, as his eyes caught her own. The marquis's fingers crept up to softly stroke her cheek, and she held her breath. He leaned toward her, and with a shiver she tilted her face up.

"Sweet Lucifer," he whispered, and abruptly yanked his hand away and turned his back on her. He cleared his throat, quite unlike the rakehell he was known to be. "Did I see you eyeing Pharaoh again this morning?"

Feeling rather ragged, Angel sagged against the mantel. "Y-yes, you did."

He strode over to the window and pushed it open, leaning out to take a deep breath. "I was under the impression that you disliked my poor horse," he said after a moment.

She managed a smile, relieved that he'd turned the conversation. "I have nothing against Pharaoh—only the price you paid for him."

James relaxed a little as well and finally turned back to face her. "My man, Algers, feels rather the same way."

Down the hall the front door opened, and the sounds of the Graham family echoed into the library. Angelique quickly headed for the door. "I should go see what they've been up to," she muttered.

"Angelique," he called after her, using her given name for the second time. "I'm sorry. That won't happen again."

"I know." She—they—had simply become caught up in the game. For Simon's sake, they could never let it happen again. Mistake or not, though, the look she had fleetingly seen in his eyes caused her to question feelings she would rather have let be—particularly the ones surrounding Simon Talbott, and whether or not she was in love with him.

"My lord, several coaches are approaching."

James looked up from his perusal of the estate ledgers and nodded at his butler. "Thank you, Simms. Alert the horde, and I'll be along in a few moments."

A minute later four pairs of feet ran past his office, to the accompanying sound of children's excited laughter and a large dog barking, and he sat back and smiled. His household, it seemed, was about to become even more boisterous. His life had given him little exposure to children, and to his surprise he was beginning to believe he had been missing something.

Yesterday, after he had witnessed his nodcock cousin kissing Angelique with all the finesse of a bull in a china shop, he had begun to wonder what might have happened if he had stayed in London and Simon had been the one to go off to war. It was fairly obvious Angelique was set on some sort of escape from her parents, and had settled on his cousin as the one to set her free. From her words in the library, it seemed she'd realized she wanted more from Simon than that. For the past few days James had been trying to visualize her in the dark rooms of Turbin Hall, and had been completely unable to conjure the image. Turbin was no place for a sprite such as Angel.

Hearing her laughter as she greeted Lily Stanfred some fifteen minutes later cheered him considerably. He noted that while he received a smile from Miss Stanfred, Simon had somehow earned an *on dit* about the girl's dressmaker and apparently found it highly amusing.

The Graham twins had young Jeremy Stanfred by the arms as they dragged him toward the stables. James herded the remaining guests inside to their respective bedchambers, and announced that they would be picnicking by the lake at noon.

That accomplished, he made his way up to the attic to recover the fishing poles he had dug out yesterday. On the way down, he paused by his grandmother's bedchamber and rapped on the door. At her acknowledgment he entered. "The Stanfreds have arrived," he told her, leaning against the door frame.

Elizabeth looked up from the dressing table as her maid finished putting up her long white hair. "I would have to be deaf or dead not to know that," she returned.

"Do you picnic with us?" he asked, grinning at her caustic words.

She grimaced. "You and your *al fresco* dining." She sighed. "As matron of the house and the only proprietor of proper behavior in the family, I suppose I must."

"Yes, Grandmama." He pushed away from the frame.

It was clear from young Jeremy Stanfred's awestruck expression, as he approached the children, that the Graham twins had been rather liberal in their description of him and of the Abbonley stables. "My lord marquis," he bowed, "I've . . . I've brought my Hannibal. Do you think you might teach us to jump like India and Henry?"

Henry leaned toward his friend. "You can call him Lord James," he whispered. "He's all the crack, Jeremy. Much more fun than most grownups."

"I believe I can manage a few more lessons," James chuckled, rumpling Henry's hair. "Care to have a go at these?" he queried, holding up the fishing poles.

"Oh, yes, Lord James!"

With that he herded Brutus and the laughing, excited children down to the picnic area his servants had prepared in the shade of a stand of elms. He found himself grinning as he watched the rest of the party arrive and sit down to eat. Abbonley had always been his place where he could be alone, though his own company was rarely comforting. Since the Grahams had arrived, the estate seemed more like a home than simply a place to escape to, and the sound of laughter and voices in the hallways reminded him of when he had been very young, before his mother had died.

The children finished eating and took the poles down by the old dock, where the ground was firmer. He couldn't see if they were catching anything, but from the shrieks of laughter he doubted it.

"You again triumph as a host," Angelique said merrily as she approached, a strawberry tart in one hand. He had noticed her fondness for the berry, and had instructed his cook to have it present at every meal. "I don't think they'll be catching anything, however." She chuckled. "Mama refused to let them dig for worms, so they have no bait."

"We'll have to see to that." James spied one of the servants approaching with a fresh platter of thin-sliced ham. "John, bring that down to the children," he instructed, "and inform them that it makes good bait."

"Yes, my lord." With a glance at him, the servant walked down to the shore. A cheer erupted as he handed the ham over to Jeremy.

"Oh, dear," Angel murmured, and he turned to look at her.

She was gazing toward the manor, and abruptly began laughing. A moment later he joined her. Grandmama Elizabeth had arrived for the picnic. Evidently, however, she had decided she had indeed had enough of dining on the ground, for trailing behind her were servants carrying, in procession, a chair, a writing table, a tablecloth and a canopy.

"She is an original," he muttered.

"Like her grandson," Angel concurred.

He looked back at her to find her hazel eyes dancing with mischief. "To which grandson are you referring?" he queried, raising an eyebrow.

"Tell me you've changed your mind about Lily," she whispered, taking a step closer.

"Tell me you've changed your mind about Simon," he murmured back, not surprised at her shocked expression. He was rather shocked that he had said it aloud, himself.

"Why should I?" she returned hotly.

"And why should I?" he repeated.

Before she could reply, Simon was there. "Come back and finish eating, Angel. Lily's been telling me an amusing story about Miss Delon which you must hear."

"Oh, by all means, excuse me," James said, sweeping a bow. "I would hate to keep you from that."

As he had expected, she scowled at him. "You certainly are puffed up with your own consequence today," she noted disdainfully, then turned away.

"Goosecap," he replied smoothly.

She whirled around and opened her mouth to make a retort. At the last moment she looked over at his cousin, snapped her jaw shut again, and with a twitch of her skirts turned to lead Simon back to where Lily waited.

James stood for a moment watching the three of them. Lily Stanfred was perhaps the more classically beautiful of the two young ladies, but there was a blithe warmth and compassion in Angelique that set her completely apart from any woman he had ever met. He only hoped Simon knew that, and that his cousin would appreciate what a rare and precious gift he had been given. With a sigh, James turned to the lake to offer his assistance to the children in their quest for supper.

9

"I've figured it out, you know."

James looked up as Simon squatted beside him. "Figured what out?" he queried uneasily, fiddling with a pebble. "Try it again, Jeremy!" he called as the boy and his gelding crossed the field they had piled with make-shift jumps.

"Miss Stanfred. I saw you eyeing her. She's why you invited the Stanfreds here, isn't she? It wasn't to aid me, it was so you could take care of your own matrimonial business."

"And?" James prompted, straightening to ease the strain on his bad leg. "Lean a little further forward, Jeremy!"

"And? And it's completely unacceptable, that's what." Simon stood to frown at his cousin.

"Why? What's wrong with arranging two marriages with one holiday? I thought it rather economical of me."

"Good God, James, you are the most cold-blooded bastard I've ever encountered. That poor girl will be like a lamb to the slaugh—"

"Why don't you stop worrying about my affairs and tend your own?" James snapped. "And start asking yourself why in the world a spitfire like Angelique Graham would want to marry a clod like you."

"I am not a clod," Simon said quietly.

James took a breath, realizing he had overstepped his

bounds. "No, you're not. Unlike myself, you are a gentleman. I apologize."

"And Angel's not a spitfire. She simply needs a husband, a household, and children to . . . settle her down. That's all."

It would be easier to blanket sunshine, James thought, but said nothing.

"Percival was appalled to hear I was coming to Abbonley," Lily told Angelique, giggling. "He insisted I would be ruined by the mere presence of the marquis."

Angel looked over her shoulder. They appeared to be alone in the garden, but she remained uncertain whether she should let Lily know of Abbonley's plans. "He's been a wonderful host," she said instead.

Lily leaned over to smell a cluster of Madame Hardy roses. "I'm always afraid to talk to him. He seems so fierce, and I just know whatever I say will be foolish, and he'll give me a set-down."

"He's not so terrible," Angelique offered.

"Not for you. You stand right up to him." Lily blushed. "I could never do that."

Angel tried to think of something comforting to say, but Lily was right. The Marquis of Abbonley was far too fierce for her, and in his striking presence she would be nothing more than a small, beautiful decoration. And, Angel realized, this whole thing was her fault. If she hadn't tried so hard to find just the wrong match for Abbonley, he might have settled on someone else entirely. Now he would look at Lily with his beautiful emerald eyes, and she would only look away.

"Ah, my two favorite ladies," Simon smiled, coming around the corner. He took their hands and brought both to his lips at the same time. "May I join you on your walk?"

"Of course." Lily smiled prettily.

Angelique glanced at her friend. "Of course," she echoed.

They strolled about the grounds for quite some time before Angel realized she hadn't heard anything from the twins or Jeremy, and she set off down to the lake to find them. There was no sign of them by the old dock, and with a sigh she started up along the north shore. A few clouds skittered across the sky, and she stopped to look out across the lake. It was beautiful here, like a small piece of paradise.

A splash several yards out into the water caught her attention. A second splash followed a moment later, but this time she saw the pebble fly overhead. She turned to see James Faring seated on the grass a short distance behind her, Brutus at his side. "What are you doing out here?" she queried, embarrassed at being found daydreaming.

"Following you," he answered promptly. "What are you doing out here?"

"Looking for the children."

"They're out behind the stable," he informed her, rising and brushing off the back of his buckskins, "plotting something I haven't been let in on yet." He motioned her back toward the manor.

"What were you following me for?" she asked.

The marquis strolled beside her, picking the bark off a twig with his fingers. "Other than the fact that you were heading off into the woods alone, I was wondering if you'd like to ride with me in the morning. If you'd like to take Pharaoh out." He flung the twig away. "I'm certain it will leave your parents insane with alarm."

She chuckled and looked over at him. His limp was nearly vanished, and a healthy tan had replaced the tired pall he had worn in Dover. Brutus trotted along at his heels, looking the very soul of domesticated obedience. "How do you do that?"

"Do what?"

"Get Brutus to listen to you. I have to offer him all sorts of bribes to get him to do anything. And he hardly listens to anyone else at all."

James laughed. "I actually don't expect anything of him. Perhaps I have the best understanding of misbehavior, and he thinks me a kindred spirit."

"And I am only a distant second in disobedience."

Abbonley shrugged, still grinning. "I suppose that depends on whose rules you are supposed to follow.'' He gestured toward the stables. ''What about Pharaoh?''

''I would be pleased to go riding with you.''

James gave a smile and nodded. ''Seven-thirty?''

''That's fine.''

He paused as they reached the edge of the trees. ''You'd best go back the rest of the way without me,'' he commented softly, ''or everyone will wonder what you and I were doing alone together in the forest.'' The Devil slowly reached out toward her, and then brushed a leaf off her sleeve, running his fingers down the patterned muslin covering her arm. ''We want you married, and not ruined now, don't we?'' he murmured.

Angelique cleared her throat, clasping her hands together to conceal the fact that they had begun shaking. ''Of course.''

''I'll go round up the children.'' He looked down at her with a slight, amused smile, then turned for the stables. Angel continued toward the house. Flirting with James Faring was quite . . . exhilarating, and she would miss it once she and Simon were married.

The table that evening was even noisier than before, despite the fact that the children, there in honor of the fact that they had provided the main course, spent most of the meal whispering and giggling to one another. They were up to something. If she couldn't discover what it was, she would ask for James's assistance. If anyone could get them to confess, it would be the marquis.

She had never seen James Faring as good-humored as he was that evening, and she spent a great deal of time watching him. He caught her gaze on several occasions, his eyes twinkling, and she could see why so many women found him attractive. By the end of the evening he even had Lily giggling, and Angel watched as her friend's parents shared a hopeful glance. The marquis's plan was apparently going better than her own, and that hardly seemed fair. The whole reason the Graham horde had come to Abbonley was so he could convince her parents to marry her off to someone else.

Angelique frowned. Not to someone else. To Simon, of course.

The next morning, the marquis was at the stables before her. It was chilly, so she had dressed in her heavy emerald riding habit with a matching hat perched rakishly on her hair. James was splendid in a black jacket and buckskin breeches, his calf-length Hessian boots shined to such perfection she could almost see her reflection in them.

"Good morning, Lady Angel," he greeted her. "Ready for a good run?"

She nodded vigorously. "Absolutely."

He threw her into the saddle, and Pharaoh turned his head to look at her. Hastings was to accompany them, but from the look James gave him as he swung up on Demon, the groom was going to be left far behind. They started off at a fast clip toward the lake, heading for the south shore. "Are we going all the way around?" she asked, urging Pharaoh even with Demon.

"If you like," he responded.

"I would."

He sent Demon into a canter, and the hunter smoothly matched them. They kept to that pace for several miles, and as predicted, Hastings dropped out of sight through the trees behind them. The morning air was fresh, and the lake through the trees glittered with the reflection of the early morning sun. When the marquis glanced over at her he had a smile on his face, and she returned it.

"This is wonderful," she laughed, tossing her head. At that her hat came loose and, before she could grab it, fell to the ground. "Oh, drat," she muttered.

The marquis pulled up. "Allow me," he offered, and yanked Demon around to head back up the path. They reached the hat, and without slowing he swung over to hang halfway out of the saddle. He scooped it up without pausing and turned to bring it back to her.

It was a spectacular piece of horsemanship, particularly on

an animal as spirited as Demon, but she wasn't about to tell him so. "Show off," she said instead.

"You have rather a lot of trouble with your hats, Angelique," he grinned, and handed it back to her.

"Only when you're present," she returned, trying to pin the thing back over her windblown hair.

"That's the first time I've been accused of causing a woman to lose her *hat*," he responded immediately. "Perhaps things are looking up for me."

She understood the insinuation and blushed, but was distracted from making a reply by her uncooperative chapeau. "Blast," she grumbled.

"Do you need assistance?" he asked, urging Demon closer.

Before she could respond he had taken the pin out of her hand and was fastening her hat back to her hair. A tingling shiver ran down her spine at his touch, and she held still so he wouldn't pull away.

"There, I think that'll do," he said after a moment. He chuckled. "In fact, you may never be able to get it off again."

She laughed and he grinned at her, his eyes merry. Her heart gave a queer flop, but then he abruptly stiffened and looked toward the lake. "What is it?"

He held up a hand to silence her. After a moment she heard Brutus's distinctive howl and then screams. Angel fell in behind James as he charged off the trail. He bellowed for Hastings to follow them, and dimly she heard the groom answer.

They cleared the trees at the edge of the lake, and she gasped. Helen and Jeremy were on shore screaming for help and pointing, while Brutus paced up and down the edge of the water, barking and yowling. Out in the water a small form thrashed, vainly trying to reach the remains of a half-sunken rowboat as it slowly drifted away.

The shore was marshy, and James dragged Demon to a halt when the horse began to fight him. He jumped down and headed for the water at a run, throwing off his jacket as he went. Helen and Jeremy flung themselves at Angel, sobbing something about finding the boat and wanting to go fishing. James dove into the water and began swimming strongly for Henry. As he reached him the boy went under, and James dove after him.

It seemed like an eternity before they surfaced again, but must only have been seconds. James had Henry tight against him, holding his head up out of the water. He stroked for the shore, Henry coughing and gagging in his grasp. Hastings appeared, and waded out toward them. When James could stand, he swung Henry up into his arms and pushed through the reeds until he reached the groom.

Hastings took Henry and carried him up to dry ground. As the groom laid him on the grass, Angel extricated herself from the children and threw herself down beside him. "Henry, are you all right?"

In answer her brother turned on his side and coughed up half a lungful of lake water, then began gasping for air and sobbing. James knelt quickly on his other side. He slapped Henry sharply between the shoulder blades, and after another gasp the boy's breathing became more even. He sat up and flung himself at the marquis's chest.

James hugged him tightly, water dripping off his dark hair and into his eyes. "Henry, I think we'd best teach you how to swim," he panted shakily.

Henry looked up at him. "Not today, please." His teeth chattered.

"Fair enough," James answered.

Steam was rising from both of them, and Angel realized they must be frightfully cold. Hastings donated his overcoat to put around Henry's shoulders. "Let's get you back to the house and dry, lad," he said, and scooped the boy up to bring him to his horse.

"Helen, Jeremy, go with them," Angel instructed, and the children ran after the groom.

In a moment they were gone. Demon and Pharaoh grazed, oblivious to the goings-on. She looked at James, soaked to the skin, his shirt muddy and steaming as the water evaporated in the warming sunlight. "Thank you," she whispered, near tears.

He started to answer, then with a startled look pulled his shirt from his breeches and then yanked it off over his head. As he threw it aside she saw the reason for his consternation. Two leeches were fastened to his skin, one on his right side over his ribs and the other on his left shoulder. With a curse he plucked them off and flung them away. They left twin bloody streaks across his skin. "Damned bloodsuckers," he cursed, then turned his back on her. "Any more?" he asked, trying to look for himself.

There was one on his back, and with shaking fingers she removed it, shuddering as she dropped it into the water. "That's all."

A deep, scarred gash puckered the skin across the back of his shoulder. She reached out to touch the wound, and felt him jump beneath her fingers. Slowly she traced the length of the scar, while he stood unmoving. Finally he turned around, his eyes glinting. James reached out both hands to cup the sides of her face, then leaned down and captured her lips with his own.

Angel's hand, still outstretched, slipped around his shoulder. His skin was cool under her fingers, but his lips seemed to burn her mouth. She shut her eyes and pulled herself up against him to meet his embrace. A shivering tingle ran down her spine. This was what she had wanted, she realized dazedly as he continued to kiss her roughly. This was what she had wanted from James Faring from the moment she had found herself in his arms on the Dover pier. She reached her other arm around his bare back, not caring what anyone would think if they happened upon her in the embrace of the half-naked Devil, but only that he would continue kissing her.

After a last fervent kiss he released her and stepped back. "Sweet heaven . . ." he muttered, staring at her as he continued to back away.

While her own face felt flushed, his was white.

"James . . ." she said slowly, wondering what in the world they were going to do now.

He shook his head. "No. This never should have happened." He backed up until he reached Demon, then turned and swung up into the saddle. "It never happened," he said fiercely, urging the stallion up beside her. "Do you understand? It never happened."

"But—" she stammered, looking up at his horrified expression.

"No. You are going to marry Simon. I will not step between the two of you. Not for anything." With that he wheeled Demon and kicked the stallion in the ribs. The two of them disappeared into the trees.

"Angel!" She jumped as Simon rode into sight on Admiral. "Are you all right?" he asked, dismounting.

"I'm not the one who almost drowned," she snapped, then took a breath, trying to gather her thoughts.

"I . . . know that," he answered. He scanned the glade around them. "Where's James?"

"He . . . um . . . had to leave," she answered slowly, half her thoughts still on their breathless embrace.

"Well, come on," Simon urged, and helped her up into her saddle. He mounted beside her. "I can't believe he rode off and left you here alone," he scowled.

"No, it was all right," she replied.

But it wasn't all right. From the Marquis of Abbonley she had just learned two things. The first was that he was no longer the blackguard he had the reputation for being, for he had been more unsettled by their embrace than she. The second thing she had learned was that she was not in love with Simon Talbott. She was in love with the Devil.

Angelique was not in love with Simon. James had suspected it earlier, but after their kiss he was certain of it. He shouldn't have kissed her at all, but he had been wanting to touch her, to hold her, for so long that he had been unable to resist. It would have been easier to stop breathing.

When he finally rode up to the stables all his guests and

most of the household staff were waiting there for him. The Grahams were practically beside themselves with gratitude, though what they would have thought had they seen him kissing their daughter, he didn't know. The attention made him uncomfortable, and he ducked away as quickly as he was able.

After he changed into some dry clothes, he summoned Algers and made immediate arrangements for the dock to be repaired and for three sturdy rowboats to be constructed. If he had taken care of it a week earlier, as he had intended, none of the morning's events would have happened. And that would have been best for all of them.

He had no intention of doing anything more about his attraction for Angel. Just because the chit had caught him off guard when she had touched him, caressed him, it didn't mean he had fallen for her. The Devil had no intention of falling for a woman ever again. Especially a copper-haired spitfire who only remembered her manners half the time.

Two mornings after the incident by the lake, he returned home from a trip to the village as Simon and Angel were preparing to go out. "Good morning, my lady, Simon," he said stiffly, as he swung out of the saddle and handed the reins over to one of the grooms. "I again offer you the loan of Pharaoh," he told Angel, "as we never finished our outing the other day."

"Pharaoh?" Simon repeated, frowning. "Why don't you simply let Angel ride Demon? Neither is appropriate for her."

It was Angel's turn to frown. "I'm certain I could handle either of them."

"I ride Demon," James said firmly. "No one else. Ever."

"That's a bit selfish, don't you think?" she queried, obviously primed for an argument.

"Not selfish," he stated flatly. "Practical. So don't get any ideas—Demon would eat you alive." He saw the stubborn light in her eyes, and frowned. The stallion was notoriously bad-tempered, and she could be hurt. "I'm serious, Angelique."

"Really, cousin. We weren't in earnest. Heaven is quite enough. Why would Angel ever wish to do such a thing as to ride that bad-tempered beast?"

Angel was bristling at Simon now as well, and James raised an eyebrow at her. She started to snap something, then with visible effort subsided. Simon turned away for a moment, and from behind his back Angel mouthed, "Beast." James chuckled.

"Care for some company?" Grandmama Elizabeth asked Simon, as she arrived from the manor. "I thought I might ride Pharaoh this morning, if you've no objection, Jamie."

"You want to ride?" James queried, lifting both eyebrows.

"I'm not dead yet, you know," she retorted. "Hastings? Saddle Pharaoh."

"Yes, milady," the groom bowed with a grin, and went to comply.

The viscountess glanced at Angel, then turned her intrigued expression on James, who turned away. His grandmother could damn well keep her curiosity to herself.

Before they managed to leave, Lily appeared, and as Simon brightened at having an ally along, another horse was saddled for her. Watching the foursome head off toward Esterley, James was unable to refrain from laughing. It seemed that Angelique was beginning to realized what being married to a proper gentleman like Simon would entail. It served her right for making such a poor choice.

"Something amusing, milord?" Hastings asked as he reappeared from the stables.

"Oh, very, Hastings," James chuckled. "Very."

He wasn't nearly as amused half an hour later when Simms came to inform him that he had callers. "Callers with luggage, my lord," the butler said dourly.

"Who?" James asked, heading for the main hallway and extremely curious about who might want to drop in uninvited at Abbonley.

"I was told to announce to you that the Alcotts had arrived,'' Simms reported grimly as he fell in behind.

"The Al—good God," James enunciated, missing a step and nearly causing Simms to run into him. "Both of them?"

"Yes, my lord."

"Good God," James repeated feelingly. Arthur Alcott was bad enough, but Percival . . . Slowly he smiled. No one seemed able to get under Angel's skin, with the exception of himself, more quickly than Percival Alcott. Now they would see who rattled whom. He flashed a grin at Simms, who for a moment actually lost control enough to look startled. "This could be fun."

10

The nasal squawk of Percival Alcott's voice sounded distantly through the passages as Angel and her riding companions entered the manor. From the noise, he was highly agitated about something. "I knew that was his coach outside," she chuckled.

"I suppose we should go see," Lily sighed.

They found the source of the noise in the drawing room. Percival stood defiantly in the middle of the floor, while the recipient of the dandy's onslaught sat in one of the chairs before the fireplace, reading and ignoring his visitor.

"Don't just sit there, Abbonley. I won't be put off," Percival fussed. "I'll know where you have her or I'll set the law on you."

The marquised looked up. "Beg pardon?"

Percival crossed his arms. "Where is Miss Stanfred?" he demanded.

The marquis caught sight of Angel through the doorway. Hooded eyes twinkling, he stood. "All right, Alcott, it's no use trying to get away with it," he said dramatically, walking to the fireplace. "She's locked in the tower. They all are."

Percival blinked, then turned bright red. "Don't try to make a fool of me, Abbonley," he sputtered.

"That's quite all right. It's no effort at all," James responded.

Angel was enjoying the play, but Lily had never had much tolerance for anyone being teased, and she freed herself from Angel's arm and walked into the room. Angelique followed behind her.

"Ah," the marquis said, coming forward, "I see you've escaped again."

"You must remember not to leave the key in the lock," Angel reprimanded him, and he grinned.

"Angel," Lily admonished, and gave a look of rebuke at the marquis.

Percival grabbed Lily's hand. "Oh, my dear Lily, you are all right. I have been so worried."

Angel started to make a sarcastic retort, but as Simon and Lady Elizabeth came into the room she changed her mind. James reseated himself, but his dancing eyes were on Lily as she extracted her hand from Percival's. For the first time Angel wished her friend didn't look so like a doll of fine porcelain.

"For heaven's sake, Alcott, what did you think had happened to her?" Simon growled, stepping between Lily and Percival.

"Who could tell, with her in the very den of the Devil?" Percival declaimed. "I had to come to see that her parents' folly in journeying here caused her no scandal."

"Ah," James murmured, less amused now at the mention of his nickname. "You've come to lend an atmosphere of propriety to my dubious household."

"Yes," Percival responded bravely.

"Well, it wasn't necessary," Simon snapped. "Miss Stanfred is perfectly safe."

Angel turned to look at Simon. Despite his bluster Percival was rather harmless, and Simon's fierceness seemed out of place. Especially when it was in the defense of someone else. It had been difficult, these past two days, since she had realized that her feelings for him weren't as strong as she had thought. Simon rushing to Lily's defense hardly made things any easier. Sometimes he was simply too chivalrous.

"Simon, if you don't mind, would you show our . . . guest

to a room?'' James suggested. His sharp eyes watched as Simon shrugged, glanced at Lily, and then guided the dandy to the door. The quick look James sent Angel was full of secrets and barely disguised passion, and she blushed and turned toward the window before anyone else saw.

The viscountess stood there looking from one of them to the other, a preoccupied expression on her face. Angel quickly turned around again, while Lily smiled and stepped closer to James.

''I'm so sorry he's come,'' she said, putting a hand out to him and making Angel want to do something unladylike.

''Not your fault, Miss Stanfred,'' James responded, smiling back at her. ''Don't trouble yourself. The more the merrier, I suppose.''

Lily sighed and smiled. ''I'd best go tell Mama and Papa who's arrived so they'll be prepared for the onslaught,'' she said, and with a curtsey left the room.

''Percival Alcott?'' Lady Elizabeth raised an eyebrow.

James nodded. ''And his brother, Arthur, is currently walking through the garden and presumably making my flowers wither.''

''Sir?'' The butler's voice came from the doorway.

''What is it, Simms?'' the marquis said.

''Mr. Algers is in your office, my lord. He's brought the post.'' He held up a silver tray containing several letters.

''Splendid. Let's have it. This one's for you, Grandmama,'' James said, handing a letter to the viscountess. Abruptly he froze and his face paled. He stood, dropping the other letters into his vacated chair, and stared at the missive in his hand.

His grandmother straightened. ''What is it?'' When the marquis didn't answer, she took a step closer. ''James, are you all right?''

James started and looked up at her, then glanced over at Angel. ''Quite.''

''Who is it from?'' Elizabeth asked.

The marquis looked down at it again. ''Desiree.''

''Jamie ...'' the dowager viscountess began, warily

watching her grandson's face. Angel couldn't put a name to the marquis's expression, but was glad to know she wasn't the cause of it.

"Excuse me." He strode out of the room, the letter clenched in his fist.

Elizabeth walked over to the window. "Five years," she muttered.

"Beg pardon?" Angel ventured.

The viscountess turned around. "I said it's been five years, and that witch still won't pull her claws out of him." She opened her own letter, then set it aside. "He and Geoffrey Pratt were friends, you know. They went to school together." She sighed. "And then, on holiday in London they attended the same ball, and met the same girl making her debut."

"Desiree," Angel supplied, wondering why she had come to dislike Desiree Kensington so strongly over the past few weeks.

"Yes. For the rest of the school year they fought over her. Almost got sent down for it, once." Elizabeth shook her head. "James was always so spirited. Very like his mother."

"What happened?"

"From the beginning Desiree played them against one another. Drove them both half mad, and they ended up hating one another. After he graduated, James proposed to her. From what I've been able to get out of him, she told him that Geoffrey had already asked for her hand, and that she couldn't decide between the two. She did point out that as Geoffrey had already inherited and was a viscount, he was of course the one her relations favored." She shook her head, her light green eyes full of regret. "I think everyone knows what happened the next morning."

Angelique looked at her. "But, Desiree?"

"James's father recommended that James leave the country. He went to France, stayed for nearly a year. Four weeks after he left, Desiree married Lord Kensington. When James heard about that . . ." Elizabeth stopped and cleared her throat. "When he came home, he was so different I barely recognized him. His reputation kept growing worse and worse, and believe me, he continued to earn it.''

''He doesn't seem so terrible to me,'' Angel offered in a small voice. And his touch, his kiss, had been anything but terrible.

Elizabeth looked at her. ''You know,'' she said slowly, ''since he came back from Belgium, James has seemed more like he used to be. The way he was before Desiree, I mean. Happier, and less angry.''

''Why do you think he's changed?''

Lady Elizabeth gave a short smile and headed for the door. ''Oh, I have my suspicions.''

James paced the library for a long while before he opened the letter. In Desiree's perfect handwriting was a short note saying she realized the time had come to explain her reasons for marrying Kensington, with the intimation that she was certain he would understand. It closed with a request to see him, and was signed, ''Love, Desiree.''

He looked at the signature for a moment, then tossed the letter into the fire. It would be like Simon or his grandmother to try to discover what Desiree was up to, for he had never been able to convince them that his relationship with her was none of their bloody business. He didn't want to see her again. There were too many other things he was trying to deal with.

He found some of those things occurring at supper that evening, and they served to brighten his mood considerably. Percival had apparently been unaware that children were present at Abbonley, and he was obviously having a difficult time reconciling this with his view of the Devil. When they all repaired to the drawing room, Alcott suggested the children be sent to bed.

At that Henry stood, drawing himself up to his full height. ''I won't have a fop telling me what to do in Lord James's house,'' he declared.

''Henry!'' Lady Niston admonished, and his father threw him a stern look.

"You told me not to lie," Henry protested to his parents. "He is a fop."

Percival pinned James with an indignant look. "This is your doing. You've corrupted these infants."

"We're not infants!" Henry shouted.

"They're not infants," James echoed mildly.

Angelique was busily engaged embroidering another handkerchief. She looked up at James, her eyes sparkling.

"I think he's a fop, too," Helen chimed in, coming to her brother's aid. "And Lord James is slap up to the echo, just like Henry says."

This time Angel's choking sounded suspiciously like laughter. James leaned forward. "Are you all right, Lady Angelique?" he asked solicitously.

"Yes, I'm fine," she managed, and covered her face with both hands.

The Graham and Stanfred parents were finally able to restore order, and exiled the children upstairs. James looked from Angelique to Simon, who was plainly displeased with her behavior, and smiled to himself. It was about time his cousin began to realize exactly what lay in store for him.

As he made his way up to bed much later, he was waylaid by his grandmother. "What's gotten into you, Jamie?" she queried as he reached the top of the stairs.

"Whatever do you mean, Grandmama?"

"It's beginning to look like a regular rout here," she stated, linking her arm through his. "I keep wondering who's going to arrive next."

He chuckled. "Shall we lay wagers?"

"Don't change the subject, you scalawag. What's going on?"

James looked down at her and shrugged. "I find it all rather domestic, in a mad sort of way."

"Jamie," she warned.

He smiled. "I don't know what you want me to tell you," he replied. "Even I must have a few scattered moments of propriety."

"But the Alcotts? You never would have tolerated them

here for a moment before . . .'' She trailed off. ''Before you came home,'' she finished.

''Perhaps I've learned patience,'' he said quietly.

''Perhaps,'' she replied, equally softly, and reached up to touch his cheek. ''And perhaps you know their presence amuses Angelique.'' She stepped into her room and shut the door behind her.

He stood looking after her for a moment. Grandmama Elizabeth was right. If he had been here alone when the Alcotts called, he would have thrown them and their baggage out in a cold Yorkshire minute. They weren't here because they annoyed Angelique. They were here because they made her laugh.

''Thank God you're here,'' Simon panted, throwing open the library door.

''What's happened?'' James asked, hoping no one else had fallen, or had been thrown, into the lake.

''It's Percival and Henry. Alcott caught the boy riding India and proceeded to lecture him on the proper mount for a youngster. Henry apparently told him to go to Hades, and then pulled off Percival's hat and had India ride over it.''

James grinned. ''And what am I to do?''

''Percival's threatening to have the boy horsewhipped if he doesn't apologize, and now Helen's gone after Alcott with that wretched doll of hers. Their parents are gone so I fetched Angel, but she only stands there laughing, and now she's got that damned slobbering Brutus baying at everyone.'' He threw himself into a chair.

James chuckled. ''So that's what I was hearing.'' He had wondered when his cousin would have enough of the high-spirited Graham family, and it seemed he'd just found out. ''Simon,'' he chuckled, ''you have the temperament of a clergyman. You also have the rather short tolerance of one, m'boy.''

''And you have the temperament of a wet cat and the tolerance of a barmaid expecting a fat vail,'' Simon snapped back at him. James burst into laughter, but his cousin scowled. "Lily tried to help, but only Jeremy listens to her. She's the only one with any manners around here, I'm beginning to believe." He flushed, then stood abruptly to pace.

"I'm pleased you like her," James said, sobering and watching his cousin closely. "I thought perhaps I'd speak to her parents at the end of the week." In truth the time James had painstakingly spent with Lily Stanfred reminded him of why he generally avoided schoolroom chits. The lady was beautiful in a classical, delicate way, and where Angel reminded him of a fox easily outwitting the hounds, Lily was like a fawn, shy and timid and needing to be protected. And, unfortunately, quite dull in comparison to the spitfire with the large mastiff who refused to leave his thoughts.

"James . . ." Simon trailed off, then abruptly stood and yanked the door open. "Go do something, will you?"

James strolled out to the stables to restore order. As he reached the yard, he motioned for Henry and India to approach. Percival was glowering, a rumpled lump of what must have been his hat on the ground beside him. The mastiff stood several yards back, all four feet braced so it could bark at full volume.

"Brutus, quiet," he ordered, and the dog gave a wag and subsided, apparently agreeable to letting James take over. "What's all this, then?" he asked.

"He says I can't ride India," Henry returned, jabbing a finger at Percival.

"I said the beast was not a proper one for a young boy to be riding, and that you should have lent him a more suitable mount," Percival corrected. "The insolent whelp then destroyed my hat."

James crossed his arms, seeing Angel off to one side shaking with laughter. "I did not lend Master Henry anything," he said flatly, keeping his expression carefully stern. "He has proven his competence, and India is his to do with as he pleases. If you touch either of them, I shall have *you* horsewhipped."

"Hurray!" Helen seconded, holding Millicent aloft like a trophy.

Percival Alcott looked rather as though he had just swallowed an insect, and after a stunned moment he stalked off to the garden, likely to help his brother kill more of the flowers. Henry dismounted and walked up to James, leading India behind him.

"Is it true?" he asked softly, his eyes shining. "Is India mine?"

James nodded. "Of course."

The boy stepped forward and hugged him around the waist. "Oh, thank you, Lord James."

James returned the embrace. "On one condition."

"Anything."

The marquis put a finger under the boy's chin and tilted his face up, so that he could look Henry in the eye. "Promise me that you'll learn how to swim."

Henry smiled and nodded. "I promise."

James led the way back to the manor while the children retold the events of the morning. He found himself once again cast in the role of their rescuer, and while Simon glowered at him, he accepted their undying admiration and gratitude good-naturedly.

"Angel, are you coming?" Simon queried.

Angelique lagged behind them, her attention on the stable yard. "Where did Brutus go?"

James stopped. "He was over by the stable a moment ago."

"I'll be along in a moment," she said, and turned around.

"Oh, for heaven's sake, Angel, he's as big as a cart. He'll turn up on his own." Simon frowned and motioned her to accompany them into the manor.

She looked at Simon, her expression hurt. "I'll be right back, Simon," she said firmly.

"Angel—"

"I'll help you look for him," James interrupted, unable to keep silent, and started back down the path with her. In a moment the rest of them, led by a scowling Simon, followed. They searched the stable and the yard, but Brutus was nowhere to be found.

"You must have hurt his feelings," Angelique accused James.

He emerged from the pile of hay he'd been digging through, and put a hand to his chest. "Me? I only asked him to be quiet," he protested.

"You two are completely mad," Simon put in from the doorway where he leaned with his arms crossed. "It's a dog. A large, loud dog. It has no feelings."

James frowned at him. Simon knew perfectly well how fond Angelique was of Brutus, and even if he believed it, it seemed a rather unkind thing to say.

"Brutus does too have feelings," Helen piped up, sticking her lower lip out in a pout.

"Simon, it will never do if Brutus thinks you don't like him," Angel pointed out with a smile which to James's eyes was obviously forced.

"It won't matter, because Brutus will not be coming to Turbin Hall."

Angelique gasped. "But—"

"I won't have that beast destroying half the Talbott family heirlooms every time he wags his tail."

James thought that some of the Talbott family heirlooms could stand to be destroyed, but he said nothing as he watched Angelique's stunned and hurt expression. His cousin was a fool to deny Angelique the simplest of the freedoms she so obviously craved, and if Simon wasn't careful he was going to lose the most exquisite thing he'd ever had in his life. A small tear began to gather in one corner of her beautiful eyes as she continued to look at his cousin.

"Lady Angelique?" James said quietly.

She looked up at him, and it was physically painful to keep himself from stepping forward and kissing the tears from her eyes.

"Yes, my lord?" she said, blushing slightly at his unguarded expression.

"There's plenty of time to worry about where Brutus will be living." He glanced again at his idiot of a cousin. "In fact, if your parents don't wish to keep him, he may stay here at Abbonley, with me."

"Then I'm staying, too," Henry said stoutly. "To make certain Brutus eats."

"Me, too," Helen chimed in. "And to make certain he gets bread. Brutus loves bread."

"I shall remember that," James commented with a slight smile.

"That's kind of you, my lord," Lily put in unexpectedly. "I have to admit, I agree with Simon. Such a large dog about makes me nervous."

Angelique's lips twitched, and for a moment her expression became amused. It seemed that neither of their intendeds wanted anything to do with the mastiff.

"Well, it's a large house," James commented carelessly. "I'm certain you and Brutus can manage to avoid one another for the remainder of your stay here."

"That's rather unkind, wouldn't you say?" Simon said shortly.

James hesitated, then nodded. "Yes, quite. Apologies, Miss Stanfred."

"Of course, my lord."

Angelique, though, was looking over at him, a question clearly in her eyes. He could guess what it was. Did he still intend to offer for Lily Stanfred, when he clearly found her so dull? Well, he didn't know yet. There was still time to decide. And since Abbonley *was* such a large house, they could probably manage to avoid one another as well for most of the time, if they wished.

"Oh, I don't care who wants Brutus next year," Angel said. "I just want to find him now."

"Jeremy and me took him walking down by the lake yesterday," Henry offered. "We saw rabbit tracks."

"He didn't want to come back to the house with us," Jeremy noted.

James nodded and rubbed his hands together. "Well, it's as good a place as any to start."

Immediately Angel stepped past Simon, who sighed and

pushed away from the wall to follow her. "Henry, show me where," she instructed her brother.

The boy nodded and hurried toward the path. "This way," he said over his shoulder.

Something touched James's hand, and he looked down to see young Helen slipping her fingers around his palm. With a surprised grin he tightened his grip and let the girl lead him down the path. Angelique turned to look behind her, and smiled at him as she noted his companion. Before he could make any comment, she and Henry disappeared into the woods. Simon and Lily lagged behind, the two of them obviously reluctant to join the hunt.

In only a moment the three groups were out of sight from one another along the twisting path, though every few minutes Henry or Angelique would call Brutus's name.

"There were more tracks over here, Lord James," Jeremy informed him, and with a nod James led the children in the direction the boy indicated.

"Brutus!" He pushed through the bushes, the children spread out on either side of him. Something tangled in the brambles caught his eye, and he squatted down. "Jeremy, Helen, stop," he ordered, and the children froze.

"Lady Angelique?" he called in a carrying voice.

"My lord?" came the response a moment later from some distance away.

"Watch Henry. There are rabbit snares here." He turned to the other two youngsters. "You two head back to the path the way we came, and watch for anything that looks like this." He indicated the thin wire and noose at his feet. An adult's foot was too large to trip one, but the children could be hurt.

"We'll be careful," Angel's reply came. "Actually, though, Henry said Hastings had told him there were bears in this area?"

James gave a short grin at the anxious tone of her voice. "Not since one escaped from the carnival ten years ago," he returned, watching as his charges carefully made their way back to the trail.

"Oh. Splendid."

Several minutes later he pushed into a small glade. Brutus sat there, one paw caught in a rabbit snare. At the sight of James, the mastiff uttered what sounded like a pained and embarrassed woof.

"You big lummox," he said affectionately, and knelt down to free him. "I don't know how competent a guard dog you are, but your hunting skills leave something to be desired." The skin above the mastiff's paw was cut a little, but he'd had enough sense to sit and wait for help rather than struggle and pull the wire tighter. James straightened and ruffled the dog's ears.

Those same ears swivelled toward the east, and at the same time James heard something that sounded very like sniffling. He wrapped his hand around Brutus's garish collar and crept slowly forward. At the edge of a small clearing he stopped, the mastiff quiet beside him.

". . . cry, Lily," came Simon's voice, and James frowned.

"But this is so wrong," Miss Stanfred answered between sniffles.

"We couldn't have known this would happen. It's not as though we planned it."

"I know, Simon, but she's my dearest friend."

At another sound James glanced quickly over his shoulder, but it was only a breeze in the leaves. He had the distinct feeling that this was a conversation Angelique should not be overhearing.

Simon sighed. "I know. And . . . well, it's worse even than that."

"What is it?"

"James," his cousin said shortly. "He's looking for a wife, and for some damned reason he seems set on you."

"Me? No!"

James raised an eyebrow. Her reaction to news of his interest seemed rather extreme, given that he had been polite and charming toward Lily Stanfred from the moment he had set eyes on her.

"I tried to convince him that the two of you would never

suit, but how could I tell him that I've fallen in love with you? And how could I ever tell Angel? She's so anxious for the two of us to marry.''

"It would break her heart, Simon." Lily sobbed again. "And you gave your word to marry her. Oh, it's hopeless.''

"Nothing's hopeless, Lily, as long as I know you love me.''

"Of course I love you, Simon. From the moment we met, I've known.''

That was followed by more sounds that James immediately identified as kissing, and he backed away from the clearing. His first, immediate inclination was to charge in and hand Simon his fist for being so stupid as to find Lily Stanfred more attractive than Angelique Graham. Only secondarily was he angry that Simon would pursue Lily, knowing his own cousin intended to marry her. He would be foolish to try to make his intentions toward Lily into something more than what they were. If he wanted a proper wife there was a plentitude of others to choose from, despite the peculiar bunch Angelique had rounded up for him.

Only then did it hit him—Simon didn't want Angelique! His mind began running in a hundred directions. He'd put himself in a hole by telling Angelique that he didn't believe in love. It would take some work to convince her otherwise. There was another problem, though, in that Simon had not yet broken the engagement. Duty bound as his cousin was, it was entirely likely he wouldn't back out of the marriage regardless of whose happiness would be ruined.

James gave a short grin. That actually could work to his advantage. At the moment, he was expected to continue flirting with her until her parents decided to save her from ruin by marrying her off to his cousin. Hopefully Simon wouldn't give in to his guilt over Lily, because if Angelique knew the truth, she might very well back away from the Devil before he had a chance to win her. She would also be hurt, knowing that Simon didn't think her proper enough to wed. If there was anything James didn't want, it was to see her hurt.

"Brutus!''

Henry's voice came from close by, and the dog gave a happy woof.

"Angel, he's over here! I heard him!"

"I have him," James called, and dimly heard the other children cheer.

This was a careful hand he'd have to play, keeping both her parents and Simon at bay. If he went too far in either direction he'd lose her. The Duke of Wellington had once told him he had a remarkable gift for strategy, but he had the feeling that this would be the most difficult battle of his life—for the simple reason that he'd never so desperately wanted, or needed, to win.

11

"**I** told you, Angel, if you see a bear, climb a tree."

Angelique grimaced and glanced about. "That's easy for you to say," she returned, pushing after her brother as they followed the sound of James's voice. "You're not wearing a dress. Besides, bears climb trees, don't they?"

"I don't know." Henry giggled. "But don't worry. I'll protect you. Lord James would be mad if I let a bear eat you."

"Don't you mean Simon would be mad?" she returned wistfully, wishing her brother were correct.

"I don't know about Simon, but Percival Alcott said you were a hoyden, and Lord James said if he ever said anything else bad about you, he would hand that fop his teeth in a bag."

Angelique's heart began hammering. "And when was this?"

"Last night." Henry paused while Angel pulled her skirt free from some brambles. "In the drawing room. I wanted to ask Lord James if he would help me teach India that bowing trick he does with Demon. You know which one?"

"Yes."

"It's a fine trick, ain't it?"

Angelique chuckled. "Yes, it is. Finish the story, Henry."

"I followed him upstairs. He stopped outside your room

127

against the railing, and just stood there in the dark, looking at your door.''

A blush crept up Angel's cheeks. She hadn't been sleeping well for the past few nights. Not since James had kissed her, in fact. The idea that he'd been standing outside her door while she lay awake in bed . . . ''I forgot to give a book to him. He was probably trying to decide whether I was still awake or not,'' she offered.

Henry made a face at her. ''I think he just likes you,'' he stated matter-of-factly. ''You should marry him.''

''Henry! I'm engaged to Simon,'' she said firmly.

''Indeed she is,'' James said cheerfully as he and Brutus emerged from the undergrowth, ''and woe is we who waited too long to woo.''

''Brutus!'' Henry ran forward and threw his arms around the mastiff, who lifted a wounded paw for examination.

''So waiting was woe?'' Angel laughed, kneeling to receive a rather damp nose in her ear and much amused by the marquis's good-humored silliness. It made her quite forget about Simon's ill-humor.

''Only for wooing.''

''But would you have wooed if you hadn't waited too wong, er, long?''

James smiled softly. ''Indeed, I would have wooed.''

Angel didn't quite know what to make of where this conversation seemed to be going, but she wished to follow it. ''But why?'' she said quietly.

Again he seemed able to read her thoughts. ''Why would I woo, or why did I wait so long to return to London?'' The emerald of his eyes was bewitching, and she didn't dare look away. ''The first should be obvious, and the second I will never forgive myself for.''

''Never?'' she whispered.

James knelt beside her. ''Never.''

''Was he caught in a rabbit snare?'' Henry queried, and Angel started and turned her eyes from James.

The marquis cleared his throat and stood. ''And the

poacher who came upon that catch would have been rather surprised.''

Henry laughed. "I'll say." He looked over at Angel as she rose. "He might even have thought he caught a *bear*."

Angel cuffed her brother lightly on the ear. "Stop that, you wicked boy," she admonished with a half-annoyed grin.

"I told you, Lord James and I would protect you," Henry replied, urging Brutus toward the path.

"We would happily dedicate our lives to such a noble cause," James elaborated with a wolfish grin.

He was obviously forgetting something. Or rather, someone. "And what does that leave for Lily?" she returned.

Annoyance crossed his sensitive features. "Whatever's necessary," he muttered.

"Not changing your mind about her, are you?" she queried off-handedly, hoping he had. For her own sake, not Lily's.

James glanced away. "I don't know," he said quietly.

It was the truth, she realized. "Well, Lily will be relieved."

"And what about you?"

"Me? Oh, I'm relieved as well. I told you she would never suit you."

He pursed his lips. "Yes, what were those requirements again? Ah, I remember. Intelligence, sense of humor, beauty, wit, charm and—what else was there?"

"You've left out demure and respectable," she offered, swallowing.

James waved a hand as though pushing those two qualities away. "That sounds rather dull, don't you think? I've decided to do away with them."

"Oh, you have, have you?"

"I have," he returned, undaunted by her tone. He tapped his chin with one long finger. "Now, who does this describe, do you think?"

"Angel," Henry answered, grinning at her.

"Henry, be quiet," she ordered, flushing.

"Do you think so, m'boy?" James jumped on her brother's comment.

"Unfortunate then, that you waited too long to woo, isn't it?" Angel cut in, and stomped ahead to walk with Brutus.

"No wedding bells have rung yet," the marquis murmured behind her, but she pretended not to hear.

She avoided James for the rest of the evening, but spent another night tossing and turning when he refused to leave her thoughts. It wasn't fair, she kept thinking, that he had been in Belgium when she'd had her Season, so that Simon was the cousin who had proposed. He didn't believe in love, she told herself over and over, James didn't believe in love and so they would never suit anyway. She would marry Simon and they would live at Turbin Hall, and she would be happy. She turned her face into her pillow so Lily next door wouldn't hear her crying. She would be happy if it killed her.

The next morning James came into the breakfast room shortly after she did. He greeted his guests, then glanced from her to Simon, his gaze far too speculative and scheming for her peace of mind, or heart.

The marquis reached for a slice of toasted bread. "As we're all gathered together, this seems a good time to announce that there is to be a ball at the Wainsmore estate on Saturday. All of the local gentry will be there," he went on, his jaw twitching with amusement, "including the rather frightening Agatha, Lady Fitzsimmons—"

"Jamie," his grandmother admonished.

"I'm not the one who saw her taking tea with her cats," James noted, and smiled as the children giggled. "Katherine and Harold wish all of my guests to attend as well."

"Ooh, a ball," Helen said excitedly, but Henry shook his head at her.

"He means all the adult guests," he corrected.

James nodded. "You're quite right, Henry, and I do apologize."

Henry grinned. "That's all right. I don't like any of that stuffy dancing, anyway."

Helen pouted. "I do."

"You don't know how to dance."

"Do too!"

"Do not!"

Simon coughed as James elbowed him in the back. "Perhaps we can arrange our own soiree," he suggested.

"Excellent idea," James seconded immediately, and Angel realized he must have been planning such a thing all along.

"And I suppose a roving band of musicians happens to be travelling through the village at this very moment?" she said coolly.

James raised an eyebrow at her. "As a matter of fact, one is. And they have agreed to play for us tonight."

"Lord James?" Helen called excitedly.

"Yes, my dear?"

Helen gestured at him, and with a slight smile he came around the table and leaned down while she whispered into his ear. Angel found it a constant source of amazement that this man, who had such an awful reputation, could be so wonderful with children.

At every turn she expected him to tire of the novelty of their presence, but he had not. Instead they had all become fast friends, and he their champion, and Angel had begun to believe that even after they returned home, she would never hear a sentence uttered by either twin that didn't include James's name. He would make a splendid father, she thought, then blushed furiously.

The marquis nodded and whispered something back to Helen, who giggled. "It's all settled, then. Our own soiree tonight, and then the Wainsmore ball on Saturday."

"Are you certain?" Angel's mother asked. "That's a great deal of trouble to go through to please the children."

"I would hope it would please you, as well," James replied. "And you should know by now, my lady, that I thrive on trouble."

Again his glance was at Angelique, and she self-consciously looked over at her parents. It was still the plan,

for him to be pretending to fall for her, but he was being
so . . . obvious about it. That was quite unlike him, and she
had to wonder if perhaps he was attempting to sabotage their
efforts. She needed to speak to Simon about it. She glanced
at him. He was scowling as Percival recited a sonnet to Lily.
Or perhaps she wouldn't. April was beginning to seem closer
than she had realized.

After much debate Angelique decided to wear her midnight blue gown, for it was her favorite. The silver ribbons
Tess wound through her mistress's long, tumbling hair
brought out its copper highlights, and as she gazed at the
confused hazel eyes looking back at her from the mirror, she
marvelled that she had let things go as far as she had. This
had to stop, for her own sanity. It didn't matter who she
loved. She had made a promise.

That resolution crumpled as soon as she made her way
down to the grand ballroom and found James lounging in
the doorway talking with his grandmother. He was dressed
all in dark grey, and as he glanced over in her direction her
breath caught in her throat. He was magnificent.

The marquis strolled over and took her hand, brushing her
knuckles with his lips. As he straightened and looked down
at her, his green eyes were twinkling and merry. "You are
breathtaking," he murmured, and kissed her hand again.

Angel felt shivery all over. Even when James Faring was
behaving, he was still wicked. "Where is Simon?" she queried. Out of the corner of her eye she noted that Lady Elizabeth was pretending not to watch the two of them, and she
tried to extract her fingers from his grip.

James ignored the attempt and instead transferred her hand
to his arm. "What do I care where he is?" he returned.
"Have no worries, though. I shall escort you inside."

Angel inhaled as they stepped into the ballroom. She had
been inside before, and had found it pretty enough, with its
tall mirrors along one wall and the large windows opening
out to the garden, but now it seemed transformed. Gold and
silver ribbons and white silk balloons and fresh roses were

everywhere, and she marvelled that James had been willing to go to so much trouble and expense.

"Do you like it?" he asked.

"It's wonderful." She beamed, feeling as she had as a child at Christmas. "Henry and Helen will adore it."

He looked down at her. "I didn't do this for Henry and Helen."

She blushed. "James, please stop this," she whispered.

"Stop what?"

"Stop paying so much attention to me," she begged.

"I'm only doing as Simon requested," he protested innocently. "You aren't becoming cow-hearted about this scheme, are you?"

She looked at him closely, completely suspicious. "So you don't mean any of the things you're saying to me?" she demanded.

"I mean them all," he murmured. "But what does that matter?"

Before she could summon an answer to that, her brother and sister charged into the room, dragging their father behind them. "I say, Lord James, is the orchestra going to play?"

"Yes, Henry. Why don't you go ask them to play us a waltz?" James said, nodding his chin toward the musicians tuning up in the corner.

Henry nodded and disengaged himself from his chuckling father to go capture Jeremy and do as he was bid. James touched Angel's fingers and freed his arm. "I have dreadfully bad manners, as you are aware, Lady Angel," he said, glancing at her father, "and I have promised this waltz to someone else."

That surprised her, but when Helen clapped her hands and pranced forward, she grinned. "Of course, my lord," she curtsied, and glanced about for her betrothed. He smiled and stepped forward. "I shall dance with Simon."

"As you should," James returned slowly, nodding at his cousin.

The orchestra struck up the waltz, and Simon led her into the dance. As they stepped about the floor, most of her attention was occupied watching James bow to Helen. They spent a moment studying her and Simon, then James took her sister's hands and they began a slow series of steps that quickly had Helen laughing, and, to her obvious delight, waltzing.

Lily and Percival joined them on the floor, as did her own parents and the Stanfreds, and then Henry walked up to Lady Elizabeth, bowed, and asked if she would care to teach him to waltz. To Angel's, and apparently James's, surprise, the dowager viscountess complied.

Angel looked up at Simon, to see that his attention was on Percival and Lily. Neither of them seemed to care that they were dancing together. "Simon, have I done something to offend you?" she asked flatly. Her looked taken aback by her bluntness, but something needed to be done.

"No. Of course not."

"For the past four days we've barely spoken except to argue about Brutus."

"That's not so," he protested, flushing.

"I think you like Lily more than you like me," she said petulantly, mostly to hear what his answer would be.

His face turned an alarming shade of crimson. "Never!" he said vehemently.

That seemed rather extreme, and she frowned. "Do you dislike her?" she asked, wondering if they had had words over something.

"Yes, of course. I mean, no." He swallowed. "I mean, this is a ridiculous conversation, Angel. Let's please talk about something else."

Angel wished with all her heart that Simon would stand up to her, make her feel as exhilarated as she did when she sparred with James. It wasn't polite to argue with a female, though, and Simon always retreated, to the point that she rather felt as though she was browbeating him. It seemed the only thing he would stand up to her about was Turbin Hall, and that was the one thing she truly wanted him to give ground on.

She looked over at James, now swinging Helen through

the air in time to the music. He was the one who understood her, understood what she wanted. He had known about her, about her tendency toward impetuous behavior, from the beginning. They were exactly alike.

The music ended, and Simon escorted her to the buffet table at one side of the room. She couldn't help but notice that again there was a large bowl of strawberries on the table. As she was lifting one to her mouth she felt someone, James, standing beside her. "Where do you find these?" she asked, indicating the berry.

He raised an eyebrow at her. "I have them smuggled in from parts distant, at great danger and expense."

"Faradiddle," she replied, grinning.

He chuckled. "Very well, you've seen through me again. They grow far out of season on the southern hillsides all around Abbonley." James took one for himself. "Though I would have them smuggled in for you, if necessary."

Music started up again, and it was Angel's turn to raise an eyebrow. "Two waltzes in a row?"

He smiled lazily. "They'll play waltzes all evening, if you wish it. No Almack patronesses here." He looked at her. "Will you dance this one with me?"

Unable to resist, or even to utter a word, she nodded and took his outstretched hand. They swept out onto the floor, and as they swirled around there was nothing but the music and James, smiling down at her.

It wasn't until the piece was half over that she noticed her parents standing at the edge of the ballroom glaring at her. She flushed and looked up at him. "They're looking," she whispered.

He smiled. "That is the idea, is it not?"

"I . . . well, I suppose . . . I don't know."

"Good," he murmured. When the waltz ended, much too soon, he led her to her parents, and then quite docilely went to fetch her a drink.

"Angel, you have been warned about that man," Camellia hissed, grim-faced.

"He's been very nice," she said stubbornly. "And he

hasn't done anything wrong, so you can't tell me he's as awful as all those silly gossips say.''

"That is beside—''

"Cammy, shh,'' her husband muttered, putting a hand on his wife's arm.

James returned and handed Angel a glass of punch, keeping one for himself. Despite his suggestion of waltzes all evening the orchestra struck up a quadrille, and Simon and Lily were trying to show the giggling children the steps.

Her father cleared his throat. "James, Cammy and I have been discussing returning home. I have my own estate to see to, and the Lord only knows what's happened to it with my man in charge.''

Angelique's heart dropped. She'd known this was only a holiday, but had managed to convince herself it would last as long as she wanted. Longer than this.

The marquis froze for a moment, then nodded and cleared his throat. He glanced at Angel. "When do you go?''

"After the ball. That will give the children five days to get used to the idea.'' Thomas grimaced. "I doubt they'll ever forgive me.''

James smiled. "I've enjoyed having you all here.''

"We've, um,'' the earl cleared his throat, "we've enjoyed being here.''

James looked as surprised as Angel felt, but before he could say anything further the twins came to drag him away for another quadrille. Angel danced with Lord Stanfred, but couldn't stop thinking that she only had five days left at Abbonley. Arthur Alcott partnered her next, but her heart was no longer in the dancing. Claiming tired feet, she sat out and tried not to mope.

"What's wrong?'' James took a seat beside her.

She shook her head. "Nothing,'' she said quietly, looking across the floor.

"How about a walk in the garden, then?''

At that she looked over at him. "At night?''

He raised a hand. "I shall behave. I swear,'' he said solemnly, though his expression was amused.

"What about Simon?"

"He's not invited."

She knew that she shouldn't go, but Angel nodded anyway, and he pulled her to her feet, tucking her hand around his arm. She couldn't help but notice how skillfully he arranged their exit, waiting until her parents' backs were turned before leading her out one of the open windows and into the garden.

There were torches scattered throughout the garden, but it was still shadowy and cool. It rather suited her mood, and for a time she strolled beside him in silence. "You didn't know your parents had decided to leave, did you?" James asked, stopping and turning to face her.

She shook her head. "No."

"And you don't want to leave?"

"No," she muttered, refusing to face him.

James was quiet for a moment. "Because of Simon, or because of me?"

Angel turned around, ready to march back inside. "I'm not going to answer that question." She glanced over her shoulder at him. "And you shouldn't be asking it."

"I know."

She sighed testily. "I know this is all a stupid game to you, anyway."

"But what if it's not?" he murmured, stepping closer to her.

For a moment Angel couldn't breathe. "It still doesn't matter. I'm engaged to Simon."

"Do you want to be?" he whispered.

Angel turned around and punched him in the shoulder. "Stop it! You said you were going to behave."

James grabbed her fist. "I'm sorry if I've hurt you, Angelique. Your damned parents weren't supposed to take you off so soon. I'm not prepared for this yet. I had everything planned out, you know. I was quite clever, I thought."

"What did you plan out?" she asked, trying to pull her hand free.

"You and me."

She jerked free. "There is no you and me! Can't you understand that? I am engaged!"

"Nothing's been announced," James murmured urgently, pursuing her as she headed back to the ballroom. "No one knows. Break the engagement."

Angelique froze. "For what? For you? You don't even believe in love."

"I love you."

Whatever it was that Angel had been about to snap at him became caught in her throat. "You can't," she whispered, staring up at his face. "I love Simon. He's—"

"No, you don't," he broke in brusquely. "You don't love Simon. I doubt you ever did."

"That is a lie." Her heart was hammering so fast she thought it must burst through her chest. This was an ambush, and it was one she had wanted. She'd wanted to hear this from James. "Is this how you talked to Desiree?" she flung back desperately. "Is this how you tried to convince her to stay away from Viscount Luester and marry you? If you don't convince me will you shoot Simon tomorrow?"

James took a step backward. He turned as if to walk away, then stopped and stood for a moment with his eyes shut. Finally he took a ragged breath and looked over at her, his eyes black in the moonlight. "I deserved that, I suppose," he murmured. "I'm sorry, Angelique." He turned his back again. "You made me forget her," he said so quietly she could barely catch the words.

"James? I'm so sorry. I shouldn't have said . . ."

He shook his head. "It was an accident, you know. I never meant to shoot Geoffrey. I certainly never meant to kill him. He was my . . ." He stopped for a moment. "He was my friend."

"Then why?"

"I went to propose to her—to Desiree. She told me Luey had already proposed to her. She said he'd told her I was . . . unreliable, that I'd never be faithful to her, and that it was entirely likely my father would cut me off without a penny for my wicked ways. She said she would rather be Viscountess Luester now than poor Mrs. Faring waiting for my father to die.''

''That must have hurt,'' Angelique said quietly.

''You have no idea. And then she said that if Luey hadn't come along she would happily have married me.'' James sat on one of the white stone benches that lined the garden path. After a hesitation, Angelique walked over to join him. ''I was furious. I called Luey out, then found Simon—dragged him out of his bed at Cambridge, in fact. We both got blistering drunk, and then I went out at dawn to meet Geoffrey.''

Angel sensed that he had never told this story to anyone, and she slowly reached out to touch his fingers. His hand jumped, and then he turned his palm to curl his long fingers around hers. ''I know what happened next,'' she said. The sound of a country dance and of laughter coming from the distant window seemed unreal.

''No, you don't,'' he returned. He raised his head to look at her. ''I truly never meant to kill him. I had already decided merely to shoot close enough to frighten the hell out of him, and perhaps convince him that he would be wise to let me have Desiree. He was as smashed as I was, and missed me by six feet. I shot him through the right lung, and he drowned in his own blood. It took several minutes.''

''And turned you into the Devil,'' Angel murmured, shivering.

''Yes.'' He looked across the moonlit garden. ''On my father's advice I went to France, and then my darling Desiree married Kensington.'' He shrugged. ''I suppose even a barony was better than what she thought she might have had with me.''

Angelique reached up to touch his cheek. He turned to looked down at her, and she leaned up to kiss him. His arms went around her, pulling her against him. This was so wrong, so very wrong, and so very right. She tangled her fingers through his black hair, wishing she could erase every memory he had of Desiree Kensington.

"Angel! Where has that girl got to, now?"

Angelique tore her mouth from James's. "Oh, no," she breathed, looking toward the manor and her father's voice. "James, let me go."

He kept his hands around her waist. "Never," he whispered, shifting over to nibble at her ear.

"Oh, my." She shivered at the sensation, which seemed to run through her entire body. "James, if you ruin me they'll send me off to Australia."

He sighed and let her loose. "I would follow you," he murmured, standing and pulling her up beside him.

"Would you?" Angelique shook herself. "Oh, never mind. Get away, please."

"Do you love me?"

"James," she begged.

"Do you love me?" he repeated huskily.

She felt compelled to answer. "Yes, but—"

"That's enough. For now." He leaned over and softly touched his lips to hers, then turned and disappeared into the darkness of the garden.

Her gown was rumpled, and she dazedly smoothed at it. If Simon had come upon them, James might have found himself embroiled in the duel he very much wanted to avoid. Something had to be done, before they all were hurt. Brutus came padding up to her, and absently she scratched his head. James loved her. And that made everything even more complicated than it had been before. She couldn't break with Simon, for she had given her word. Once James had suggested it, though, she found it impossible to banish the notion from her thoughts. Oh, her parents were right. She was entirely incapable of behaving in a proper and mature manner.

Something rustled in the bushes to her left, and she whipped around, her heart pounding. She saw nothing, and when Brutus sauntered over to root among the leaves she thought perhaps it had been a rabbit or a mouse. When he emerged, there was something dangling from his massive jaws. Whatever it was caught the moonlight and glinted.

"Brutus, give," she ordered, holding out her hand, and he dropped his prize into her palm. It was a monocle. She lifted it for closer inspection, and her heart skipped a beat. The gold rim was engraved with the initials P.A.

12

James Faring didn't sleep at all. He'd been about as subtle as a bee sting with Angelique. A green boy just down from university would have performed a seduction with more panache than he had. The only comfort was that Angelique had said she loved him. True, there were a multitude of conditions and complications attached, and he'd practically beaten the confession out of her, but she'd said it.

It was her damned parents' fault. He'd thought to have at least another fortnight to wheedle her away from her thoughts of Simon, during which time he would have gently broken the news that his cousin was in love with Lily Stanfred.

It did cross his mind to simply sit back and hope that Simon would summon enough impropriety to call off the marriage, but there were two reasons he couldn't risk that. Firstly, Simon's sense of honor was so deeply entrenched that it had likely never occurred to his cousin that he could change his mind. And second, Angelique was no one's cast-off, and he would never allow her to be treated as such.

She didn't appear for breakfast, and he found himself as angry at Simon for apparently not noticing her absence as he was at himself for upsetting her enough to keep her away. He went down to the stables in time to see Simon and Lily riding off toward the lake together. "Damned insensitive . . ."

Heaven was in the near paddock as Angel appeared from the direction of the garden. She cooed at the mare and produced a lump of sugar, while James quietly stepped forward to lean against the railing a few yards from her. Several strands of her long hair had escaped from their pins, and unconsciously she pulled them back behind one ear with her fingers. She was wearing a light green patterned muslin, a shawl knotted over her shoulders against the cool morning, and he would always remember every detail of her.

Heaven finished the treat and then trotted back to the far side of the paddock. Demon stood crowded up against the railing of the neighboring corral, his neck craned in Heaven's direction and his ears tipped forward at the mare. "It seems Demon has aspirations to reach Heaven," he offered.

Angel turned to look at him. "So it seems," she returned, with a smile. "You pun well."

"Thank you," he answered, smiling back. "I have to admit I can sympathize with my poor beast's yen for so divine a creature." James ventured a step closer, but wasn't surprised when she raised a hand as if to ward him off. She'd had a night to regain her sensibilities. And if she had any sense she would club him over the head and run for assistance.

"Stay right there," she ordered, blushing. "Do not begin this again."

"But last night—"

"Last night we were seen," she interrupted.

Good Lord, he'd ruined her. "Who was it?" he murmured, wishing he could kiss the troubled furrow from her brow.

She fished something from her pocket. "I heard rustling in the bushes, and Brutus brought me this."

He stepped forward, and she deposited a monocle in his hand. "Percival Alcott," James said darkly. He looked up at her. "Are you certain he didn't simply drop this on another occasion? He and his brother have been tramping about my garden for days.''

She shook her head, turning back to the corral. ''With the way this entire scheme has been proceeding, what do you think?''

''Hm,'' the marquis murmured. ''You're right. But he doesn't know you're engaged, Angelique.''

She sighed and lowered her head. ''That doesn't matter. I've been behaving like such a hoyden. No wonder my parents are concerned.''

James reached out and lifted her chin. ''I've been doing my damndest to seduce you,'' he murmured. ''And believe me, I've had a great deal of practice. It's no fault of yours, Angelique.''

''It *is* my fault,'' she protested. ''I wanted you to seduce me. I still do.''

James gave a slow smile. ''I'm glad to hear that.''

He leaned forward, but she put a hand against his chest. ''No.''

''Well, we seem to be in a bit of a spot, then,'' he commented, running his thumb along her cheekbone. ''What do you suggest we do?''

She shivered. ''Nothing.''

He raised an eyebrow, surprised. ''Nothing?''

''When a lady is given a choice between being involved in a scandal and doing nothing, she does nothing,'' Angelique informed him firmly.

''And who told you that?''

''My mother.''

''Ah. I should have guessed.'' James glanced toward the corral where Demon eyed Heaven longingly. ''Well, my sweet, you may be a lady, but, as I have been told on numerous occasions, I am no gentleman. And this Devil has no intention of letting you go that easily.''

''James—''

''Break the engagement, Angelique. Be with me.''

''Be with you how?''

''Any way you wish,'' he returned, his voice quite unsteady. "Though I would suggest marriage as a reasonable choice."

For a long moment she simply looked at him. "But what about . . . what about Simon?" she whispered.

She was giving in, he realized joyfully. "I'm certain he'll make do."

"But he loves—"

James tilted her chin up further and stopped the rest of her protest with his lips. Her hand, which had been resting against his chest, wrapped around the lapel of his jacket and pulled him against her, and he knew he'd won. He could tell her, about Simon and Lily.

"Angel!"

At the sound of her mother's voice Angel jerked away from him. Her face turned alarmingly white. James cursed as Lady Niston, led by Percival Alcott and followed by his grandmother, strode across the grass toward them.

"Mama," Angelique stammered.

"You see?" Percival sniffed, "I told you this would happen in the Devil's den."

Reflexively James reached out to steady Angelique, but at her appalled look he stilled his hand. Instead he turned to her mother, prepared to take as much of the blame as she cared to confer. "Lady Niston," he drawled, "I was merely demonstrating how Lady Angel might wish to proceed with Simon. It seems she has little experience with—"

"Not a word!" her mother growled. Lady Niston grabbed Angelique's arm and dragged the girl back toward the manor. "You . . . devil! Stay away from her!"

"Yes, my lady," James bowed, though he had no intention of doing any such thing.

Angelique expected to be bellowed at for lowering herself to behave in such a completely disgraceful manner. Instead her mother glared at her, tight-lipped, and then suggested she go up to her bedchamber and wait. As soon as Angel shut the door behind her she ran to the window, to see James standing out by the corral where she had left him.

A light breeze lifted the dark hair from his brow as he stood looking out over the lake. He looked so alone, and her heart ached. She should never have let herself fall in love with the Devil Marquis of Abbonley. Nearly anyone else would have been acceptable if she had changed her mind about Simon, but not him. The irony was, that without James Faring, she would probably still be deluding herself into believing that she could force herself to be happy in Simon's idea of proper life.

As if sensing her gaze, he turned and looked up at her window. If she were Juliet and he Romeo, she would expect him to climb up and rescue her. She sighed, pressing her palm against the cool glass. There was no balcony, and no trellis, and at the moment even the problems of the Capulets and Montagues seemed more manageable than what faced her and James.

The marquis turned as his grandmother approached. They spoke for a brief moment, James obviously agitated. He started toward the house, but Lady Elizabeth grabbed his arm and said something more to him. He stopped and looked down at his grandmother, turned to look up at Angel again, and then strode for the stables and vanished inside.

By the time her mother pushed open her door it was late afternoon, and Angel was beginning to wonder whether she should try an escape, and where in the world she would go if she managed to get away. Her heart was here, with James. She would simply have to hope her parents would understand. And perhaps Simon would forgive her some day.

"Mama," she began, rising.

"Not a word," her mother snapped. "Come with me."

Apprehensive, Angel followed her mother down to the drawing room. She was surprised to see that her father and Lady Elizabeth were already there, waiting. Simon and James were in attendance as well, standing at opposite ends of the room and obviously trying to ignore one another.

"Angelique, your father and I have discussed your behavior over the past two months. We were wrong to bring you here, so some of what has happened rests on our heads, as well.'' Lady Niston gestured at her husband, who glanced at Angel and James and then cleared his throat. He didn't look entirely comfortable with the proceedings. Perhaps he could be reasoned with, when her mother wasn't about.

Lady Niston continued. ''We have decided to return to Niston as we planned. And, in light of today's incident, we have decided to delay the wedding until next September.''

''Papa,'' Angel protested. Things were becoming completely out of hand. ''I need to talk—''

''It's too late for talking, Angel,'' her mother cut in. ''Simon, an hour ago we posted a letter to London announcing the engagement of our daughter to you. That should clear up any future . . . misunderstandings.''

James shifted, every muscle tense and his expression angry, but he kept his silence.

''You've . . . announced the engagement?'' Angel said faintly when no one else appeared to want to speak.

''It should be in the paper by the time we leave for Niston.''

That was the end of it, then. The end of James, and the end of what she had begun to hope would be a truly happy life. She looked over at Abbonley, but he wouldn't meet her gaze. After a moment he turned and strode out of the room, shoving the door shut behind him with a slam that rattled the windows.

He wasn't at supper that evening. Angel wondered where he might be, but was soon distracted and annoyed by the smug gaze Percival had for everyone at the table. Simon had said nothing to her since the announcement, but he looked dismayed. She couldn't blame him. She had behaved abominably. As soon as she could, she would ask his forgiveness and try to make a new start of things. Lily looked as though she had been crying, and Angel thought it kind of her to be so concerned over this mess. Henry ate almost none of the meal, though it was roast chicken, his favorite.

After dinner, as they repaired to the music room to listen to Lily and Arthur Alcott play, Henry intercepted her. Taking her by the hand, he dragged her into the morning room. "Percival says you and Simon are really going to get married," her brother said, a tear running down his face.

"Henry," she murmured, kneeling in front of him.

"You can't marry Simon," he said brokenly. "He's the wrong one. You have to marry Lord James."

She hugged him, wishing with all her heart that things could be that simple. "Henry, I've been engaged to Simon all along. You know that," she whispered.

He nodded, wiping at his eyes. "But it's still wrong."

"Marrying James would be wrong, when I've already made a promise to Simon." She tousled his hair. "It'll be all right, Henry."

"No, it won't. Lord James is mad, and he won't ever want to see us again."

"Whether he wants to see me or not, Henry, of course he'll want to see you and Helen. You know that."

She rose to go into the music room, then stopped and sighed. She'd had her fill of everyone's looks and opinions. "Henry, will you tell everyone I have a headache and have gone to lie down?"

He nodded. "All right, Angel."

Feeling far too restless for bed, Angel instead headed for the library. The door was closed and so she knocked. When there was no answer she pushed the heavy oak door open and closed it behind her, taking a breath as she entered the cheery room. All she had wanted was freedom from convention. She had never counted on falling in love with the most unconventional man in London.

"Tired of the celebration already?" a voice came from behind her, and she started and turned around.

At first she didn't see James, for the only light in the room came from the dying fire, but then he turned up the lamp in the corner where he sat. She immediately sensed that something was wrong, and as he took a long swallow from the snifter he held, watching her over the rim, she realized what it was. He had been drinking, and from the small amount of brandy left in the decanter on the table beside him and the glassy glitter in his eyes, had been drinking quite a bit.

"I thought you'd stopped that," she said, gesturing.

"Ah, but this is a special occasion," he sneered, taking another swallow. "We failed to get you wed by the end of the year, but you have your announcement now, don't you?"

"You know that wasn't what I wanted."

He stood and moved toward her. "Wasn't it?" he snarled. She backed away, uncertain how to deal with the Devil in this state. "Please, I'd like to leave." Her back came up against the wall next to the window, and she was forced to stop.

"You will have a proper marriage, live in a proper house and raise proper children," he continued, moving still closer. "But will you feel like this?"

He leaned down and kissed her roughly. Trapped as she was between the wall and the marquis there was nowhere she could go, but it didn't matter. Angel didn't want to get away. Her arms went up around his neck, while his hands at her back pulled her closer against him, molding her body against his and reminding her of how tall and strong he was. His lips tasted of sweet brandy.

Slowly he broke the kiss, and looked down at her with those emerald eyes. He held her close against him, and she leaned into his body. They would think of some solution. There had to be something. Anything, as long as she could be with James.

"Very sweet," he murmured. "Do you feel that way when Simon kisses you?"

She tensed, and he kissed her again. "That's not fair," she shivered when she could breathe again.

He gave a little bow. "I specialize in being cruel and unfair." He walked rather unsteadily over to the mantel, and she was reminded that he was quite drunk. "Your parents handled that rather well, don't you think?"

"What do you mean?" she asked suspiciously.

"They maneuvered right around any steps our sterling Simon might have taken to back out of marrying their hoyden of a daughter," he explained in a husky voice.

"Hoyden?" she snapped, stalking up to him.

"That's right, Angelique," he breathed. "Wasn't that the plan? You've made your bed," he murmured, and gave a soft, humorless chuckle. "Now you have to lie in it. Literally."

Angel slapped him. "If you weren't a drunken . . . pig, you would know what a fool you are," she spat, tears running down her face. "I hate you."

His hand trembling a little, James reached up to touch his lip. "Tears right on cue," he muttered, looking down at the blood on his fingers. "You're learning. I suppose I shan't be invited to your wedding now, sweetling?"

"That's right," she answered. "You're not invited."

With that she turned and fled the room. She had thought she loved him, and that he cared for her. What a gudgeon she was! He was as cruel and heartless as she had heard. She would never forgive him.

"Angel, what's wrong now?"

Crying as she was, she hadn't seen her parents talking at the head of the stairs. "Nothing," she sobbed, pushing past them to enter her bedchamber. "Everything."

"Cammy," Niston began, but his wife raised a hand.

"I know what is best for our daughter, Thomas," she said. "And he'd never marry her. He'd only ruin her." She turned and entered their own bedchamber.

"I wonder," the earl muttered, looking at his daughter's door for a moment before he followed the countess.

James awoke at his desk in the study. From the glare through the curtains it was morning, and if he needed any proof that he'd had too much to drink, his throbbing skull made it clear enough. He groaned and straightened. Every muscle was stiff, the inside of his cheek cut against his teeth where Angel had slapped him. Five years as the Devil had provided him with a good repertoire of insults and enough deep anger to use them. It was just unfortunate it hadn't worked.

Oh, she was angry, all right, and she packed quite a punch for such a petite thing. He had wanted to convince himself that Angelique was wrong for him, that they would never suit, and to show her that she was right to marry someone else. Instead he had only hurt both of them, for the shock and pain in her eyes had felt like another wound deep inside. And all of his insults and accusations still hadn't managed to change one apparently inescapable fact—that he was desperately in love with Angelique Graham.

A quiet scratch came at the door, his skull reverberating with the sound. "Come in," he whispered.

Apparently he had made himself heard, for his grandmother opened the door and peered in. "Good God," she exclaimed, then lowered her voice at James's flinch. "I thought you'd given that up," she muttered, entering.

"I changed my mind," James replied hoarsely. "Don't worry yourself."

"Jamie, after all this time worrying about you is part of my character."

"That's your problem," James murmured.

"Not very polite this morning, are you?"

"I've given it up," he returned flatly. "The whole damned pretense of respectability. I've no use for it."

Elizabeth took a seat in one of the chairs facing the desk. "So that's it then, is it? We're back to the drinking and carousing and that miserable existence you used to pretend amused you?"

"I'm not in the mood for this conversation," he snapped.

"Then change it," she said unsympathetically. "Change everything."

He glanced up at her. "And you are referring to—what?"

"The engagement, of course."

James closed both eyes. "Oh. That."

Elizabeth leaned forward, putting her face level with his. "What are you going to do about it?"

"Do?" he repeated bitterly. "I believe the Grahams have already taken care of *doing* what needed to be done."

"You're going to let them marry, then."

With effort James managed to stand. "What do you suggest I do, Grandmama, call Simon out? That's how I handle these things, isn't it? He can have the chit, and be done with both of them."

"But you love her."

"That mannerless hoyden? Not likely," he lied, avoiding her eyes. "You have your grandsons confused."

She sat back and glared at him. "Perhaps I do. Yesterday you were ready to storm into Angelique's room and make away with her, and today I find you whining and moping in defeat."

"Yesterday," he pointed out succinctly, "the engagement hadn't been announced."

"So that's the way you're going to leave it."

"Yes. I'm fully capable of making my own decisions and living my own life, miserable and lonely as you may consider it." James looked away. "And I think that when the Grahams and Stanfreds leave, perhaps you and Simon should as well."

"No."

"I don't believe I gave you a choice, Grandmam—"

"No. After your mother died, your father became a complete hermit. If he'd cared about anything, he might have done better by you. Angel isn't dead. This isn't over. Not by a—"

"It is over," he snapped. "Simon will give her a better life than I could, anyway."

Elizabeth stood and turned for the door. "Bah. I've seen you hurt, and I've seen you angry. But until this moment, I've never seen you quit."

"Then don't look," he grunted.

A short time later James made his way upstairs and into the practiced care of his valet. He came down afterward to learn he had missed breakfast, which was actually a relief. When he went out to the lake to see how the dock was progressing, he found the children there before him.

He stayed out longer than he had time for, knowing full well he was doing so in order to avoid seeing Angelique.

Perhaps that would make it easier, to know she hated him and wouldn't have him even if she could. He sighed irritably, tearing an innocent blade of grass to shreds with his fingertips. Nothing would make it easier.

13

Angelique spent the night imagining all sorts of dastardly things to do to James Faring, and was disgusted when she couldn't come up with anything clever enough to suit. She might be a hoyden, but the last person who had any right to criticize her for it was the Devil. "Oh, hellfire," she muttered as she left her room to head downstairs.

"You don't appear to be pleased," Simon said, coming up to meet her.

"I'm surprised you're even speaking to me," Angelique said, stepping forward to put a hand on his arm. "I've been awful to you. I'm so sorry."

Simon shook his head. "James has led far less naive women than you astray," he said. "And I haven't been . . . entirely honest with you, either."

"You haven't?" she prompted when he paused, wondering who, exactly, James had bothered to trouble himself with leading astray.

"No." He took a breath. "But that hardly matters now, does it? We will be married. And all of our silly plotting and scheming has done nothing but cause trouble, and a further delay." At the landing he paused again. "I should simply have known better than to include James in this. He thrives on setting everything on its ear. The sooner we all depart Abbonley, the better."

"You're leaving as well?"

"James rather insisted that Grandmama and I leave when you do." He shrugged. "It's just as well, for I have no real wish to remain here with him, anyway."

Angelique gave a sniff. "Nor do I."

"I mean, I love him dearly," Simon went on, throwing out one arm, "but he's always been so damned . . . wild. He knew we were engaged. And he should have stayed away from you." He looked away and cleared his throat. "Has he said anything further to you about Lily?"

"I think he's decided against offering for her," Angel replied somewhat stiffly. She was furious at James, but relations between the cousins were strained enough without her adding fuel to the fire by telling Simon precisely what had transpired between James and her.

"Good."

Everyone else was at luncheon when they arrived outside. Lily's eyes were red and puffy, and Angel wondered if she had caught a cold. Angel had spent far too little time with her friend, and far too much with James Faring. Simon greeted Lily, his manner quite subdued, and his eyes closely studying her friend's face. Angelique frowned. The expression on his face rather reminded her of the way James had looked at her. Until last night, anyway.

Before she could dwell further on that, Henry grabbed her elbow. "I saved a place for you," he said.

Angel sighed. "All right." She allowed herself to be led to the table that seated the remainder of the guests, and paused for a moment to greet Lady Elizabeth, who looked about as ecstatic about events as she felt. When she realized to which seat she was being led she tried to balk, but it was too late to do so without making a scene.

Henry pulled her chair out for her, and James stood stiffly, something she couldn't read flashing in his eyes. "Good day, my lady."

"My lord," she answered, sitting opposite him.

She looked down and started her lunch, intent on finishing and leaving without saying another word. Before she had taken her second bite, however, Henry began kicking her leg. She ignored it, then kicked back. Nothing worked.

"Henry, stop it," she hissed.

Her brother was giving her such grimaces that for a moment she thought he was choking. Reflexively she glanced at James, who was eyeing Henry curiously. He had touched none of his lunch, and she thought with grim satisfaction that he must have quite a head after last evening.

"What is it?" she finally asked, hoping her ankle wasn't bruised.

Her brother gave an audible sigh and shook his head, obviously feeling he was dealing with a complete imbecile. "We're going fishing this afternoon. Do you want to come with us?"

"I don't think so, thank you," she said stiffly, bending her head again.

"But we're not using worms. Lord James, tell her she should go with us."

"I would think Lady Angelique would want to spend time with her betrothed," James muttered tonelessly, spearing a dark glance at his cousin.

Angel glared at him. "I do not need you to tell me the proper way to conduct myself," she said, angrily popping a strawberry into her mouth.

"Is that so," James supplied in a voice that made her shudder.

"It is so," she murmured fiercely, "and so is this. You had no right to do or say any of the things you did last night. You have only yourself to blame for your unhappiness."

"I see," he replied, his voice calm but his eyes glaring at her.

The children were staring from one of them to the other, dismayed.

Angel stood, drawing herself up to her full height. "And if I were a man," she spat, "I would have called you out over your behavior."

As soon as she said the words she regretted them. James came to his feet so quickly his chair fell over. Mostly to give herself time, for she was certain he would come after her, she threw her plate at him. It hit him squarely in the chest, the contents running down the front of his fine gray coat.

"Angel!" her mother gasped, as the rest of the guests sat frozen with shock.

Angel ignored her mother and backed away from James, but after shooting her a look of almost uncontrolled anger he turned and strode for the manor. As he passed the serving table, he picked up a large crystal punch bowl and threw it at the wall. It hit with a resounding crash and shattered. The marquis didn't even slow down.

"What did he do to you last night?" Simon snapped, stepping up beside her and grabbing her arm.

"He was just very rude," she said, her voice trembling. "But what do you expect from the Devil?" she continued, and fled.

She ended up in the garden, and after making certain that Arthur and his fop of a brother were nowhere to be seen, she sat beneath an oak tree and sobbed. On the far side of the manor Demon whinnied, no doubt annoyed at being led out for exercise so close to his meal time. She straightened, wiping at her eyes. She would show the Devil how much she thought of him.

"What do you wish me to do with this, my lord?" James's valet queried, lifting the food-covered coat off the floor with two offended fingers.

"I don't give a damn, Perry. Burn it." James shrugged into a clean coat, his thoughts so much on Angelique that it took him a moment to realize that, for once, dressing hadn't hurt. Being furious had its merits, after all.

"A waste, my lord," Perry commented, grimacing.

Simms scratched at the door. "My lord?"

"What?" he snarled, stalking over to yank it open.

His butler's startled expression quickly set itself to one of distress. "My lord," he said in a voice even more dour than usual. "My lord, you have a caller."

There were far too many people at Abbonley already, as far as he was concerned. "Well, who is it?"

Simms cleared his throat. "Lady Kensington, my lord."

The blood drained from James's face, and he had a sudden urge to take a seat. He resisted, instead staring at his butler and willing him to confess that it had been a joke. A very little joke. "Is she alone?"

"Yes, my lord."

"Well. I'd best go see what she wants, then."

His mouth dry, he followed Simms to the drawing room. The butler would have opened the door, but James impatiently motioned him away. He took a breath and pushed it open. Desiree, clad in a dark burgundy gown, stood by the window looking out toward the lake. Her long black hair was pulled back by combs, the trailing ends curling down over one shoulder. Fleetingly, he wondered if she still smelled of lavender.

She turned around. "James," she breathed, "I knew you would see me."

With feigned composure James strolled over to lean against the mantel. "You're not the most likely visitor I can think of. What brings you to Abbonley?"

"Didn't you get my note?" she asked, coming closer with a rustle of skirts.

"I did," he replied. "And you heard what I said to you in London."

"Yes. And I wanted to explain things to you," she said, running her fingers along the back of the couch.

"So you said."

"It's been so long since we've spoken, I scarcely know where to begin."

James tilted his head, trying to read her expression. "Begin with why you married Lord Kensington four weeks after I killed a man for you, why don't you," he suggested.

"I never told you to kill anyone," she returned.

"Sweet Lucifer, Desiree," he swore, "you did everything but put a pistol in my hand."

Desiree looked at him for a moment. "My aunt and uncle

wanted me to marry Luey," she said softly. "I always wanted you. I still do."

"You've a funny way of showing it," he retorted.

"You mean by my marrying Clarence."

"Very astute."

"James, you didn't used to be so cruel," she chastised coolly.

"I didn't used to loathe you," he returned bluntly.

Desiree's fingers stopped tracing patterns on the back of the couch. "After I got over my shock at the news that you had actually killed Geoffrey, I real—"

"You were flattered," he broke in, listening to her tone, "that I did it."

"Who wouldn't be?" she returned. "What's more romantic than a duel?"

"Flowers." The fingers had begun moving again. "At least no one need die over posies."

"Let me finish, love," she suggested. "I realized that my aunt would immediately try to marry me off in order to reduce the scandal. You had fled to France, so—"

"So you married Kensington."

She smiled the beautiful smile that had once induced even him to attempt poetry. "Yes. When I married Clarence," she began, "he was so old I thought for certain he'd have died by the time your father allowed you to return from your banish—"

"Of overexertion, I presume?" James suggested coolly.

"Oh, of something, James," she returned, clearly annoyed at his interruptions. "And then I would be a wealthy widow, and you and I could have had anything we wanted. Don't you see?"

"I begin to," James muttered. And he had thought himself cold-blooded. "Though you might have considered that I could have afforded to give you anything you might have wished for, myself. You might have waited for my return."

"Your father would have cut you off in a minute if you'd married me after that."

"Ah," James said, examining his nails, "so my wealth and title do figure into this somewhere."

"Of course they do," she snapped. "I'm not a fool, you know."

"No. You're not. But I was." A fool to ever have become tangled in Desiree Langley's arms.

"You begin to understand, then," she murmured, misunderstanding. "And you see what troubles me now. Clarence hasn't died, even after five years. Every night I see that wrinkled old man in my bed, when it should be you."

"Ah," he muttered, waiting to hear what abomination would next come from those ruby lips.

"But now we can be together. We were meant to be together," she whispered, and leaned up to kiss him.

That kiss answered one question. He was no longer in love with Desiree. In fact, what he felt most strongly was revulsion. "Am I to kill him, then?" he asked slowly.

"Of course not." She kissed him again. "We'll be in London all winter."

"And?" he murmured, hearing his grandmother calling his name.

"There's no reason you couldn't spend the winter at Faring House in town."

For a long moment he looked down at her. "I've been away from Abbonley for two years, Desiree. I think I should like to spend the winter here."

She returned his gaze. "Who is she?" she asked after a moment. She continued to look at him. "That girl from the ball, isn't it? I thought I recognized that look. You used to look at me that way. Angel Graham, yes?"

"It's no concern of—"

"I've been hearing for the past year how desperately her parents wish her to settle down and become proper. Do you really think you're the one to do that?"

"People change, Desiree."

She shook her head, giving a small, sensuous smile. "No, they don't. Your cousin was courting her as well, wasn't he? Tsk, tsk, James. I'm beginning to believe you can only be interested in a woman someone else possesses." She looked at him from beneath her lashes. "Which still leaves me, my Devil."

"Lord James!" Henry called from somewhere close by.

He took her proffered hands. "People do change. If I've learned nothing else in five years, I do know better than to listen to anything which flows past that forked tongue of yours."

"James," she protested, trying to pull free.

He released her. "I may not be the one for Angelique, but neither am I so foolish as to wish to share your bed, you viper. Get out of my house, Desiree. I never want to set eyes on you again."

"But you love me," she protested.

He shook his head. "I loved you once. I do not any longer." There was someone else he loved, someone whom he would never have, both because of his own stupidity and because of the woman standing in front of him. "Get out, before I have you thrown out."

"You wouldn't," she gasped.

He looked at her for a long moment, trying to figure out what he had seen in her five years ago to make him ever do such a thing as kill someone to win her affection. "No," he said, considering. "I'll do it myself."

He grabbed her arm and pulled her toward the door. She began shrieking as he yanked it open and dragged her into the hallway. "Simms!" he bellowed, and without a word the butler pulled open the front door. James dragged Desiree onto the drive beside her coach, and then let her go. She fell on her backside, still cursing at him, and very little resembling the beautiful ornament he had once found so infatuating. "Fly away on your broomstick, witch, before someone burns you at the stake."

He turned around and strode back inside, and Simms slammed the door behind him with a gratifying thud. Elizabeth and a wide-eyed Henry stood beside the butler.

"Thank God you've that much sense left, anyway," his

grandmother said, waving her bone fan in front of her face.
She was quite out of breath.

"It did feel rather . . . satisfying," he conceded.

"Well, you have another worry at the moment."

"And what might that be?"

Lady Elizabeth swung her fan toward the back of the
manor, nearly cracking it against the side of her grandson's
head. "That girl has gone mad," she announced.

James looked in the direction she indicated. "Angelique?"

She grabbed his sleeve and tugged him forward. "You
must go to the stables at once, before it's too late."

"Shouldn't you be complaining to Simon?"

"He'd never understand. Go!" She turned and hurried for
the stairs. "I'll get the smelling salts," she called over her
shoulder. "Simms!" she bellowed.

James took a moment to grin down at Henry. "I do believe
Grandmama has bats in her belfry."

Henry giggled. "I like her," he whispered.

He nodded. "So do I. And I think I'd best go see what
your sister is up to."

Angelique had been right when she had called him a fool.
None of this was her fault, or even Simon's fault. It was his
own. For the first time he knew what love, real love, was,
and he couldn't have it.

Desiree had been right about one thing. He was still the
Devil, and he could think of no reason in the world why
Angelique would want him, even if he hadn't behaved like
a complete boor. She would certainly gain no respectability
from him. As he came around the corner he was nearly run
down by Toombs, the assistant groom.

"Oh, my lord," the groom panted, "thank God. I tried to
stop her, but she got around me and let India and Admiral
out, and I had to fetch them back."

James gave a reluctant smile. "Outflanked you, did she?"

"My lord, you don't understand. She rode off, and I
couldn't stop her."

"Unescorted?" James asked, frowning. It was a bit late

in the day to go off riding, much less without an attendant. "Where's Hastings?"

"Oh, Lady Elizabeth sent him off on an errand. But you don't understand."

"Understand what, man?" James demanded, exasperated.

"She rode off on *your* horse," Toombs announced, backing away.

"*What?*"

The groom nodded, swallowing. "She rode off on Demon."

"That little hoyden," James cursed. So that was what Grandmama Elizabeth had been talking about. "Saddle Pharaoh. Now."

"Yes, my lord."

Too impatient to wait, James followed Toombs into the stable and quickly helped him rig out the hunter. "Which way did she go?" he barked, swinging into the saddle.

"Toward the village, my lord."

James kicked Pharaoh and lay flat along the stallion's withers as they passed under the low door of the stable. Angel had a good head start, and if Demon hadn't thrown her and she was lying somewhere with her neck broken, he would be hard pressed to catch her. His heart pounding, he urged the bay into a gallop and headed east over the low rise.

In a few minutes he spotted them far ahead under the scattered trees. Demon had clearly taken the bit in his teeth and was heading toward thicker forest, where he would have an easy time scraping Angelique off on some low-hanging branch and heading home in time for his oats. Brutus pounded beside them, trying to keep up but no doubt doing more harm than good. A yowling dog was hardly the thing to put Demon back in good spirits.

Angel, riding astride with her skirts hiked up, managed to haul the stallion into a turn that would take them back to the meadow. James yanked Pharaoh around to head them off. As they cleared the trees she saw him, and choosing the most practical, and dangerous, option, she let go the reins and tumbled out of the saddle. She rolled a few feet in the long grass, then lay still.

"Angelique!"

James reached her and threw himself out of the saddle, terrified she had broken her neck after all. He wasn't prepared for the absolute terror that jolted through him at the thought that she might be hurt. It seemed that no matter what his mind told him would be best to do, his heart refused to give up the idea that he loved her more than he'd ever loved anyone in his life.

As he knelt beside her, Angel slowly sat up to brush grass and leaves off the front of her habit.

"Are you all right?" he asked urgently.

"No," she answered calmly, examining the soiled hem of her skirt. "I've torn my dress." With that she began sobbing, wrapping her arms around her knees. He put a hand on her shoulder, but she shoved away from him. "Don't touch me."

"You might have been killed," he said, furtively plucking leaves off her back.

"Oh, it was stupid, stupid, stupid," she sobbed, rocking back and forth. "I should have known you would have a beastly, ill-mannered horse."

"If you hadn't gotten on you wouldn't have fallen off," he pointed out.

"I didn't fall," Angel retorted, her pride apparently intact. "I jumped."

"It seems to have had about the same result," James said dryly. "I warned you about Demon."

"I thought you were showing off," she said flatly. "I didn't come out here to be rescued."

"Then why did you steal my horse, ride out here, and, ah, jump off?"

"I didn't steal him," she retorted, keeping her face turned away. "I just wanted to show you."

"Show me what?"

"That you're not always right about everything."

"Hm. Well, apparently I was right about Demon," he returned in the same tone.

She shot him a quick, angry look. There was dirt smudged on her nose, and he thought she had never looked more beautiful. "Go away," she sniffed.

"Go away?" he repeated densely.

"I don't wish to speak with you any longer."

So she still hated him. He had done an excellent job of that, anyway. "I can't very well leave you out here, and you couldn't ride Demon back even if you wanted, because he's halfway to the stables by now."

"Then I'll take Pharaoh."

"I'm not walking," he said flatly. Her hair had come loose from its pins, and as he plucked grass out of it, he barely resisted the urge to run his fingers through the long tresses.

"How very ungallant of you," she sniffed, wiping at her eyes.

He flinched, and hoped she didn't notice. "You said you didn't come out here to be rescued," he reminded her. "I'm only doing as you wish."

"Go away, or I shall . . ."

"Shall what?" he pursued, curious as to what she would threaten him with.

She bowed her head. "I don't know," she muttered, then straightened again. "But it shall be dreadful," she warned.

"I have no doubt it shall be." He rose and despite her protests pulled her up after him. She swayed unsteadily, but refused his offer of support. Instead she shoved at him, and turned her back.

Brutus had been sitting to one side, and as James took an angry step forward, the dog stood and growled at him. "Oh, *et tu, Brute*?" he grunted.

"Good dog," Angelique encouraged, but that apparently convinced Brutus that everything was fine again, for his ears came forward and he wagged his tail.

"I'm sorry," James said mockingly. "Perhaps I should have let you fall on your head. Maybe that would have knocked some sense into you."

"Into me?" she said indignantly, turning to face him again. "I'm not the drunken pig."

"No," James retorted, "you're the ill-mannered hoyden."
She swung her fist at his face, but this time he was ready.
He intercepted her wrist, holding it firmly in his fingers. They
spent a moment glaring at one another, and then she jerked
free, and with a flounce of her skirts started across the
meadow with an indignant limp. "What do you think you're
doing?" he asked, grabbing Pharaoh's reins to follow.

"I'm going back," she snapped over her shoulder.

Because of the tall grass she had to lift her skirts to her
knees, and despite the fact that he was angry enough to spit,
he had to enjoy the view. It was no good being a rake if one
couldn't admire a beautiful woman, whatever the circumstances. "Oh," he said, trying to cool his temper. "Well,
I'm heading the same way. Care to ride double?"

"No."

She continued toward the manor, and he slowly drew even
with her, certain she would give in and agree to ride the rest
of the way. In accordance with her well-documented stub-
bornness, however, she never even gave Pharaoh a longing
glance.

It made him feel rather unchivalrous, and he cleared his
throat. "Angelique?"

"I'm not speaking to you."

"You've said that already."

"Good. I'm pleased to know you're not deaf."

"I'm trying to apologize," he pursued through clenched
teeth. "If you love Simon, I wish you to know I won't . . .
interfere in your lives." He desperately wanted to tell her
about Simon and Lily, but it was no longer any of his
damned business. "And I wish you all happiness."

"How gallant," she muttered, staring at him for a moment
before she turned away again. "If I cared what you wished."

Finally, James decided, it was safe to conclude that things
couldn't possibly be any worse.

14

"That was quite a spill you took, Miss Angel," Tess said as she lay Angel's blue muslin over the back of a chair. "Your habit is a sight. Are you all right?"

"I only hurt my pride," Angel replied glumly, examining her ruined skirt.

It had not gone at all as she had planned. She had thought to show James Faring that . . . well, something that would let him know she wasn't to be trifled with. Considering that Demon had nearly torn her arms out of their sockets and that she had a twisted ankle and scratches up and down her arms, she wasn't certain who had been taught a lesson.

Railing at James as she had, made her feel like a complete shrew. It was either keep herself furious at him, though, or throw herself into his arms and destroy what little scrap of respectability remained to her. Everything was so confusing. James Faring had stolen her heart, and she had no idea how to recover it, or how to make do without it.

Sitting upstairs and missing dinner seemed rather childish, but she was in no mood to see the disappointed looks her mother and father would share as they shook their heads over their incorrigible daughter. Angelique straightened. Perhaps if she behaved badly enough they would call the wedding off altogether. After a moment she slumped. She had no wish to be sent off to Australia with Brutus, and that was beginning to seem the next step down from where she had set herself.

Finally, she limped downstairs to find Simon and apologize for her latest misbehavior. Before she could find him, though, he found her.

"Can I speak to you for a moment?" he said in a quiet voice, coming out of the morning room and glancing up and down the hallway.

"Of course. I need to speak to you, as well." She stepped inside, turning to watch as he shut the door. "I know I've been behaving abominably," she grimaced, "And I'm truly sorry. It's just that—"

"My behavior has been even worse." Simon faced her, his expression solemn and anxious.

"What do you mean?" she queried, turning to find a seat. To her surprise Lily was there as well, seated by the fire.

"It's nothing you've done. I want you to know that. I've always known of your . . . high spirits. The problem is, well, it's me. You and I are friends, but—"

Angel groaned. "I knew I'd ruined everything."

Simon took her hand. "No, Angel. It's not you. Truly. I've . . . oh, damnation," he swore uncharacteristically, and turned a pleading look on Lily.

"Angel, we didn't mean it to happen," Lily said, taking her other hand.

"For what to happen?" Angel demanded, confused. The two of them looked at one another again, and then she knew. "Oooh . . . "

"I won't back out of our marriage," Simon said hurriedly, his expression tortured. "I gave my word to you. I just, well, I couldn't say nothing. It wouldn't be fair."

"You love Lily," Angel said slowly, looking from one to the other. "And Lily loves you."

"Oh, Angel, I feel so awful," Lily said mournfully, tears welling in her eyes. "I know how you feel about Simon, and—"

"It's all right," Angel said firmly, giving a small smile. "Really, it's all right." She wasn't certain what one was supposed to feel upon hearing this sort of news, but she was fairly certain it wasn't relief. That, however, was exactly what she was feeling.

Simon shut his eyes. "I'm relieved you understand," he muttered. "Lily and I have decided we will never see one another again. I will make this up to you, Angel. I promise."

"We both will," Lily sniffed, wiping at her eyes.

"Simon, I can't marry you," Angel said. "I won't even attempt to blame it on you and Lily, because to be perfectly honest, I'm happy for you."

"But then, why?"

"I don't love you," she said simply.

"You don't—" Simon sat back and looked at her. "James."

Angel blushed. "What do you mean?"

"You love him, don't you?"

Her blush deepened. "Simon—"

"Don't you?" he pursued.

"Yes," she scowled, for it was quite a troublesome circumstance, and growing more so by the minute.

He sighed. "He won't give you any respectability."

"I know."

"And he claims to have sworn off love." He looked down for a moment. "Even with all of the things he's said about Desiree, when she arrived here today I truly wasn't certain whether he'd turn her away or not. I'm—"

Angel gasped. "What? Desiree was here?"

Simon nodded. "Grandmama said she wanted James back." He gave a small smile. "He refused. Adamantly, from what I heard."

"He *is* over her, then!" Angel looked over at her companions and cleared her throat. "He said he was," she explained, embarrassed.

"I wonder why?" Simon murmured.

"Well, at the moment we're not even speaking, so I have no idea," Angel commented ruefully. She sat forward and rubbed her hands together. "But what do we do about the two of you?"

"Nothing."

"That's no answer," she protested, having heard enough of that word. "You must break the engagement."

"But that will cause a scandal for you," Simon argued, paling.

"Then I shall."

Simon grabbed her hand again. "Angel, you mustn't. Even if there wasn't the obstacle of the announcement, Lily's parents have become convinced that James will offer for her. I cannot compare to a marquis, and certainly not to one as propertied and wealthy as James."

"So elope."

It was Lily's turn to gasp. "Angel. That's so—"

"Scandalous?" Angel finished. "You love one another. For heaven's sake, show a little spirit."

"But if we're stopped on the way to Scotland, just the two of us . . . " Lily shuddered.

"You mean you would consider it?" Simon asked eagerly, kneeling at Lily's feet.

"Well, if it weren't so improper," Lily said slowly, "but I don't think I could begin my life with you under such circumstances."

Angel sat for a moment, tallying up how many things she had done wrong since James Faring had explosively come into her life. It hardly seemed as though it could get any worse. "What if I were to be your chaperon?" she suggested.

"Oh, Angel, I couldn't ask such a thing," Lily protested.

"Would you?" Simon interjected. "Would you help us?"

Angelique smiled. "Of course."

Simon grinned in obvious relief. "Thank you." His look became more uncertain. "So how do we go about this?"

Angel sighed. "Do I have to take care of everything?" she grumbled. "Simon, go have the carriage made ready, then pack yourself a valise. Lily and I will do the same, and we'll meet you at the stables in," she looked at the clock on the mantel, "one hour."

"An hour?" Lily repeated, her face pale.

"Unless you've changed your mind," Simon said hurriedly, taking Lily's hands.

She smiled. "No." She leaned up and kissed him. "One hour."

Angel hurried into the kitchen and stole a napkin of bread, for she was rather hungry, then rushed upstairs into her own bedchamber to pack. Apparently thinking it was bedtime, Brutus padded in and jumped up on the foot of her bed, where he proceeded to wallow on her best cloak.

"Brutus, get off of there," she ordered, tugging at it. He woofed at her and rolled over on his back. She gave a reluctant grin. "Brutus, please, I'm trying to make an escape. You must get off." That produced no better results, and she sighed. "You always listen to James," she complained. "Why won't you listen to me?"

At the sound of the marquis's name, the mastiff sat up and wagged his tail, then jumped off the bed. "You like James, don't you?" she murmured, tears unexpectedly filling her eyes. "You'll be happy here at Abbonley, then, because I really don't think Mama wants you about." She would have been happy here, as well, and angrily she wiped at her tears. If she had dreamed of a place to spend the rest of her life, it would have been Abbonley, and the man she spent it with would have been James. She had been such a shrew to him, though, and he had been so angry with her.

She closed her valise and started for the door to fetch Lily, but stopped when Brutus came away from the window to follow her. "No, Brutus," she said. "Now you may lie on the bed."

He tried to push by her, and with another sigh Angelique pulled a piece of bread out of her pocket and tossed it on the floor for him. When he pounced on it she slammed the door on him.

Simon's own carriage driver was waiting in his seat when they arrived out at the stables. Hastings's assistant, Toombs, was standing by the horses and watching them suspiciously. "Ready?" Simon said, coming away from the door to help Lily into the carriage. His hands were shaking, and Angel reflected that she was likely the only one who was going to enjoy the adventure.

"Yes," she smiled, and glanced over at Toombs. "Are you certain the Wainsmores wanted us to take tea tonight?"

"The—oh, yes, they were quite specific," Simon returned with a nervous smile.

"Hey, Angel, where are you going?" Henry called, running down from the manor.

"Oh, drat," Angel muttered. "We're going to see the Wainsmores, Henry. We'll be back before midnight."

"Why?"

"A poetry reading," Angel improvised.

"Oh," Henry returned, obviously disappointed. He watched as Simon helped her into the coach and then climbed in behind her.

"Go into the house, Henry," she ordered him. "It's cold out here."

Simon signalled his driver, and they headed off toward the main road. "That's odd," Toombs muttered, looking after them.

"What's odd?" Henry queried.

"Wainsmore Hall is the other direction. They're heading for the north road."

"Jamie, you're being an abominable host."

James looked up from the estate books and raised an eyebrow. "Am I?"

His grandmother stepped the rest of the way into the library. "You are. So quit sulking and go entertain your guests."

"I'm not sulking," he returned.

"What do you call it, then?"

"I'm being contemplative."

His grandmother snorted. "I have no sympathy for you any longer. If you refuse to take my advice, then the results are your own stubborn fault."

"Your advice being for me to kill Simon and make off with his intended, I presume?"

"Jamie, you know full well that—"

"I already followed your damned advice once," James interrupted, slamming the book shut. "You told me to fall in love with someone. Well, I have, and I'm much, much happier now. Thank you, Grandmama."

"Jamie—"

"I'm trying to be civilized about this," he growled, "and at the moment the best way for me to do that would seem to be to stay away from her. Go talk to Simon. He's won the day, so let him be the bloody host for one night."

"I already tried that. I can't find him."

"Well, perhaps he's with Lil—Angelique," he offered with a frown. "They are engaged, after all."

Someone scratched at the door. "My lord, Lady Elizabeth," Hastings said, stepping into the room.

James stood. "Good God, Hastings, what happened to you?"

The groom was covered with road dust and grime, and looked as though he hadn't slept in days. "Just back from running an errand for Lady Elizabeth, my lord," Hastings returned, and pulled a letter from his coat to hand to the viscountess.

Elizabeth turned it over to read the address, then touched the groom's arm. "Thank you, Hastings. You said you would make it in time, and you have."

The groom grinned and doffed his hat at her. "I'm a man of my word, my lady," he said, and with a bow stepped back out of the room and shut the door.

"What is it?" James queried.

She looked at it again, then handed it over. "Merry Christmas, James," she said quietly.

He frowned as he accepted the letter. "A bit early for the holidays, isn't . . ." He looked at the address and then shot a startled look at his grandmother. "This is addressed to the London Times."

"Yes, I believe it is."

James abruptly took a seat. "It's the announcement, isn't it?"

"I would think so," she returned dryly.

James shot to his feet again. "But Grandmama, you could go to prison for this!"

"For daft Lady Niston trusting such an important missive to the London Mail? I think not."

James grinned. "There'll be no announcement on Monday," he said softly. "I can apologize for being such a boor, and perhaps she'll—"

"She'll admit she still loves you?" Elizabeth supplied.

"I do hope so." His smile faded. "There is still a complication. Simon."

"Simon will manage without her. I'm not so certain about y—"

"Lord James!"

James sent a frown in his grandmother's direction at the sound of Henry's voice. "What now?" he muttered.

"I shudder to consider," she returned.

He stepped to the door and pulled it open. "What is it, Henry?" he queried.

The boy grabbed his hand. "Quick," he said, panting. "You have to hurry!"

"Hurry where? Did Angelique steal Demon again?"

"No! He stole her!"

James raised an eyebrow. "Demon stole Angel?"

"No! Simon stole Angel!"

"What?"

Henry released his hand. "Angel said they were going to the Wainsmores, but then Toombs said they were going the wrong way and taking the north road."

"The north road?" James repeated. There was nothing of real interest for a hundred miles along the north road, until it hooked up with the road to—

"Gretna Green," came Lord Niston's grim voice from the doorway.

"Oh, no, Thomas," Lady Niston whispered, clutching her husband's arm.

"I told you we never should have made them wait that

extra time," Thomas growled. "We should have known she'd never sit still for it."

"And now you've damned her to a miserable life with my stuffy cousin," James spat, clutching at the letter.

"What's going on?" Percival Alcott queried, sticking his head into the room.

"Simon and Angel have eloped," Elizabeth supplied, her eyes on her grandson.

James jammed the letter into his pocket. "No, they damn well have not," he snarled, and pushed past Alcott. "Have Toombs saddle Demon!" he yelled over his shoulder.

He took the stairs two at a time, ignoring the ache in his leg. From the landing he could hear Brutus scratching at Angelique's door, and as soon as he'd found his greatcoat and gloves he headed for her bedchamber. When he yanked open the door the mastiff reared up on his shoulders. "Brutus, come," he said, turning for the stairs.

Elizabeth was at the stables when he and Brutus entered. "James, calm down," she ordered.

He pushed by her and grabbed Demon's reins. "I will bloody well not calm down," he retorted. Elizabeth started to protest, and he swung up into the saddle. "You can't have it both ways, Grandmama. And I've made *my* decision. She's not marrying Simon."

"James!" she called after him, as he whistled at Brutus and kicked Demon in the ribs. "James!"

Bumping along the road to Scotland was not nearly as fun as Angelique had thought it would be. Of course, if she'd had someone to hold hands with she might have felt differently, but it was swiftly beginning to look as though being Lily and Simon's chaperon was going to be quite dull. She sighed and crossed her arms.

"Do you think they've missed us yet?" Lily queried, giving an anxious look out the window into the darkness.

"Probably," Angel responded, "though by the time they figure out exactly what's happened, we'll be too far along for them to catch up."

"You think they'll pursue us?" Lily asked faintly.

"I doubt it, Lily," Simon comforted. "I'm certain your parents will understand eventually, and no one would have any reason to follow me."

"Or me," Angel said forlornly. Something faint and vaguely familiar came to her ears, and she looked toward the window. "Do you hear something?"

Simon looked over at her. "Like what?"

"I don't know." Faintly over the rolling meadows the sound came again. "Barking?"

"It's probably the Earl of Dusson, running his hounds."

Angel raised an eyebrow. "In the middle of the night?" The noise came again, louder, and Simon frowned.

"Definitely hounds," he muttered. "Maybe they got loose."

Angel shook her head. "I know that sound." It came again, from quite nearby, and she frowned. "Oh, no."

"What?" Lily quavered.

"It's Brutus."

"I thought you closed that damned beast up," Simon snapped.

"I did," she protested. "Someone must have let him out."

"Well, he's not coming with us."

"Oh, yes he—"

"Stop that bloody coach!"

Angel jumped at James's stentorian bellow. Her heart began hammering.

"James?" Simon queried, and leaned up to bang on the ceiling. "Stop the coach, Wicking."

"Aye, sir."

"What in the world does he think he's doing?" Simon grumbled, unlatching the door as the coach rolled to a halt.

"You don't think he's after me, do you?" Lily stammered.

Simon looked back at her as he pushed open the door. "I don't think so, Lil—"

He disappeared from view, closely followed by the sound of a body hitting the grass. With a gasp Angelique rushed to the door. Abbonley stood over his cousin, his face in the moonlight a mask of wounded fury. "James," she said, jumping to the ground.

James raised his head. "I know you were angry at me," he growled, "but by God, Angelique, would you really marry him just to spite me?"

That was it, she abruptly realized. Henry hadn't seen Lily climb into the coach. Everyone thought it was just the two of them. James was jealous. The Devil was jealous, and that was marvelous. "James," she began, taking a step forward, "it's not—"

"It's not any of your damned affair," Simon cut in, pushing to his feet.

"You made it my affair, when you sent me after your woman," James snarled.

"She doesn't want you, James. Can't you see that?"

"Simon," Angel protested, appalled. "I can speak for myself."

Abbonley looked at her for a long moment. "I don't blame her for not wanting me," he said slowly, otherwise ignoring his cousin. "I just don't want her to be miserable because of me."

"You came after me?" she whispered.

"Of course I did. Angelique, I love you." He reached out as though to touch her, then lowered his hand again. "But even if you don't love me, you deserve to be with someone who will make you happy. More than anything else, I want you to be happy. I never want to see that sparkle leave your eyes."

"Oh, James," she murmured.

"Now just a moment!" Simon protested indignantly, red-faced. "What's going on here?"

"Angelique is not going to marry you," James informed him, dangerous wariness running across his features.

"I know that. Why in Lucifer's name did you drag me out of my coach and threaten to beat me to death?"

"So you wouldn't—"

"You didn't beat him, did you?" Lily gasped, climbing down from the coach and flouncing forward to confront

James. "You evil, evil man!" She punched him in the chest.

James raised a hand and took a step backward, his look completely befuddled. "Will someone please explain what's going on here?" He eyed Lily warily.

Angelique stifled a grin. "Simon and Lily are eloping to Gretna Green," she said. "I'm chaperoning them."

James blinked. "You're eloping with *Lily*?" he repeated, turning on his cousin.

"Yes, I am."

"I knew you were mooning over her, but you, *you*, are actually eloping with someone you're not supposed to be with?"

It was Angel's turn to scowl. "What do you mean, you knew he was mooning over Lily?"

"I, ah, heard them, when we were looking for Brutus."

Angel stalked up to him. "And you didn't tell me?"

James stood his ground. "I wanted to make you fall in love with me, first."

"I was already in love with you."

"You were?" Simon queried.

"You were?" James echoed softly.

"I was. But then you were so awful to me . . ." Tears began to fill her eyes, and she angrily blinked them away.

"Angelique," he murmured.

"And then Simon told me Desiree came to Abbonley to see you."

"She did. But all I could think of was you."

Simon cleared his throat. "Angel, we can't stay here all night. Come on." He gestured her back at the coach.

"Angelique, don't leave," James whispered.

She turned to look back at him. "I . . . I gave my word I'd go with them. To lessen the scandal."

James pulled a missive out of his pocket and tossed it at Simon. "There's no scandal except what they cause for themselves."

Simon looked down at the parchment. "The announcement?" he exclaimed.

"Grandmama stole it. There's no engagement." He put

out a hand and wrapped his fingers around Angelique's arm. "This is your decision, and you're going to have to do it on your own. Angelique's not going to Scotland with you."

"Yes, I am."

"No, you're not."

Simon and Lily looked at one another, and after a moment Lily nodded. "We'll go back with you," Simon said. "We'll do it right."

Angel wanted to ride back to Abbonley with James, and she rather thought that was what he wanted, as well. Simon's more proper sense prevailed, though, and so she and Brutus climbed into the coach and they turned back for Abbonley. Simon and Lily seemed much relieved at having avoided a scandal, but all Angel could think of was James riding out in the dark beside them.

It was nearly dawn when they turned back up toward Abbonley. Every window was blazing with light, and all of the guests and members of the household seemed to have crowded into the yard as James dismounted and pulled open the door of the coach.

"You brought them back," Angel's mother sobbed. "Thank you, my lord."

James shook his head. "They brought themselves back."

Apparently everyone had realized Lily's absence as well, and another hour of explanations and apologies followed. At first Lily's parents seemed less than pleased by the ordeal, but when pressed about his interest in her, James pleaded baffled ignorance, a sterling performance, Angel thought, and after that everything seemed to fall into place quite well. Except where she was concerned.

James had said that he loved her, but when they all repaired to the dining room for a hurried breakfast, he vanished. Amid all of the congratulations being offered to Lily and Simon, she was beginning to feel quite put out. Even Percival's nearly hysterical ravings over Lily did little to cheer her up.

Angel couldn't stifle the tears that kept welling in her eyes. "Oh, bother," she muttered, surreptitiously wiping at them.

She raised her head to find Lady Elizabeth looking at her. "I'm becoming such a watering pot," she complained, forcing a smile.

"Nonsense. When someone sensible as you cries, there's always a reason."

"Sensible? Me?"

"Yes, you. You know, my dear, I was thinking how foolish my grandson must be feeling right now, knowing what it must have looked like when he went galloping after you when you weren't even eloping. Especially after the fight the two of you had."

"He wasn't foolish," Angel stated. "He was romantic."

"Hmm. Even so, it might take our devilish marquis quite some time to decide whether or not he is worthy of you. You, however, are supposed to be leaving Abbonley in two days." Elizabeth smiled. "They say all is fair in love and war. I'm not certain what you two are facing, but I think you would have a wonderful time together finding out."

Angelique stared at her. It was actually quite a simple solution, if she had the courage to do it. "Where is he?"

The viscountess's smile broadened. "In the library, hiding." She squeezed Angelique's hand. "And you didn't hear that from me."

Angelique smiled and stood.

"Where are you going, Angel?" her mother queried.

"I asked her to fetch me a shawl," Lady Elizabeth supplied, and motioned Angel out the door.

Angel nearly stopped in her tracks when her father gave her a small nod and a wink. He knew, but then he'd always had a better understanding of her than her mother had. "I'll be right back," she said with a grin.

The library door was closed, but with a deep breath she opened it and barged in. James was throwing pieces of parchment one by one into the fireplace. He jumped as she entered, then smiled. "Angelique." He picked up the remaining pile of papers and tossed them onto the flames.

"Letters?" she queried.

He nodded. "To and from Desiree. It seemed well past time to get rid of the damned things."

"After what she did to you, I can think of something I'd like to send her," she snarled. "Something poisonous."

"Steady, Galahad," James grinned, crossing his arms over his chest. "There's no more rescuing to be done today." He grimaced. "And I rather botched last night, as well. I should have realized. If I know anything, it's that you're no fool."

Angel shut the door behind her and took another breath. It had to be now, or she'd never get up the nerve again. "Do you like children, James?"

He frowned and tilted his head at her, his gaze alone making her feel weak-kneed. "Children? If they're like your brother and sister, yes, I like them. Very much. Why?"

She nodded, pursing her lips, and torn between amusement and terror. "How about the theater? Do you like theater?"

This time he raised an eyebrow. "I'm not overly fond of Johnson," he said, "but I rather like the opera."

Again Angel nodded. "As do I. And horses?"

"I'm quite fond of horses." James's emerald eyes were dancing, and she thought he was catching on. "I also like strawberries, and am developing a decided fondness for a certain large brown mastiff."

He wasn't trying to escape, anyway. Angel clasped her hands behind her and rocked back on her heels. "Well, in that case, my lord, I think—"

Shaking his head and frowning, James stepped forward and put his hand over her mouth. "No, you don't, Angelique. Sit down."

"But—"

"Down."

"I don't want—"

James grabbed her arm, dragged her over to the couch, and sat her down on it. "After everything you and I have been through," he said, "I'll take care of this, if you don't mind."

He sank down onto one knee in front of her and took her hands. His own were shaking. It was then she knew everything would be all right. He looked up into her eyes for a long time, then briefly lowered his head.

"Angelique," he said, looking up at her again, "I have been accused of many things, most of which I have done. I am quite willing to try my hand at respectability, but cannot guarantee my success." He smiled at her. "I have a new list of requirements, and I've built it around you. You are the most enchanting, bright, beautiful, outrageous woman I have ever met. I am desperate to spend the rest of my life with you, but if you do not wish to risk your reputation by being with me, I will understand. Angelique, I love you with all my heart. Will you be my wife?"

It was the most heartfelt, touching thing she could ever have hoped to hear, and again tears filled her eyes. "I love you, James. And I have virtually no reputation to risk. Yes, I will be your wife."

Chuckling, James stood and pulled her up against him. She stood on her tiptoes, and he captured her lips with his own. She thought the kisses he had given her before had been passionate, but as he enfolded her in his arms and transferred his kisses to her hair, cheeks, and throat, she had a glimpse of what married life with him was likely to be. The thought delighted her.

"Hurray!"

James jumped, and they turned to see Henry skip into the room. He wore a grin so wide, Angel wondered that his cheeks didn't split. "Henry," she admonished breathlessly, James's arms still close around her.

"You are finally getting married?" Henry demanded.

James nodded and quickly kissed Angel again. "Yes, we are."

"So you're my brother?"

"As soon as we are husband and wife, I will be," James answered, grinning. "And I'm not waiting till next September, either."

"No?" she whispered, for she and Simon had never thought of attempting to set their own date.

"No. How do you feel about being a winter bride?"

"Yes." She chuckled.

"And I can come to Abbonley as often as I wish?" Henry pursued, charging about the room.

"Henry, get out," James said, and kissed Angelique again.

"But can I?" Henry tugged at James's sleeve.

Angel giggled.

"Good God," the marquis muttered, "are all children like this?"

"I hope so," Angel answered gleefully.

"I say, aren't you going to answer me? You ain't married yet, Angel."

James let Angelique go and intercepted Henry as he circled happily around them. He lifted the laughing boy up into his arms, carried him over to the window, and while Angelique laughed so hard tears ran down her cheeks, put him outside and pulled the glass shut.

"Now, my love," James said, striding back over to her and sweeping her around in a breathless circle before he bent his head to kiss her again. "Where were we?"

Avon Romances—
the best in exceptional authors and unforgettable novels!